I0664285

GEORG OLANO

Reflective Existence

First edition

Editing by Kate Cardone

This book was professionally typeset on Reedsy.
Find out more at reedsy.com

Contents

Introduction

Stories have always been part of who I am — not as a trained writer, but as someone who needed to bring certain ideas to life. This book would not exist without the support and encouragement of the people around me.

First, I must thank my wife and editor, Kate, whose belief in me has been constant. She has been my anchor through every challenge, every doubt, and every late night spent shaping this world.

Without her, none of this would have been possible.

I also want to acknowledge the writers whose visions shaped my imagination long before I ever considered writing myself. The cyberpunk authors of the 1980s and 1990s opened windows into alternate futures — gritty, vivid, and alarmingly plausible.

This series is my tribute to those creators: the dreamers who showed us neon skies, rain-slicked streets, and the fragile humanity surviving within them.

I like to imagine my work as one of those well-worn paperbacks you might stumble upon at a secondhand bookshop — a little faded, a little frayed, but still alive with possibility.

To my beta readers — Julian, Beth, John, Helen, Peter, Lucio, and Cassandra — thank you for lending your sharp eyes, your insights, and your encouragement.

There are pieces of your spirit woven into these pages.

Finally, a word of thanks to a piece of technology that feels almost lifted from the very genre I love — ChatGPT, an AI language model that became a tireless sounding board as I developed these stories. In some ways, collaborating with it felt like stepping directly into the world I was trying to create.

Thank you for taking this journey with me.

I hope these pages offer you a glimpse into another existence — one not so far from our own.

1

Chapter 1: Genesis of QUEST

Amber adjusted her stool, aligning herself with the desktop camera for her video log. The clean room, pristine and clinical, hummed faintly with the sound of air filtration systems. A sparse, white workbench stretched across one wall, its sterility broken only by the video log workstation. Opposite, data storage cells and charging docks glowed faintly, a constellation of tiny LEDs reflecting off the polished surfaces. Through a large viewing panel, the adjacent main lab bustled with quiet energy, the faint sounds of machinery underscoring the hum of progress. "Subject eleven, rattus norvegicus domestica test, complete. The procedure was successful." Amber's voice was calm, precise. She paused, letting the weight of the words settle. "We achieved full neural pattern transfer from a biological brain to its synthetic substrate. This process involved mapping the neural patterns and synaptic connections of the original brain, digitising them into a quantum-compatible format, and integrating them into the synthetic neural network of QUEST 0.9 (Quantum-Unified Encoding for Synaptic Transfer)."Amber's lips parted slightly, as if to say more, She

3

exhaled, fingers drumming lightly against the workstation's surface. At sixty two, Amber carried the weight of decades in her sharp brown eyes and measured tone. A scientist with a storied career, she had spent her life pioneering the frontier of her fields, pushing boundaries where others hesitated. She was methodical, brilliant, and relentless, but the years had worn on her. Deep lines marked her once soft brown skin, more from exhaustion than age, and silver streaks ran through her tightly braided hair. The pursuit of knowledge had cost her— long nights spent refining the project, and the gnawing ache of what had been left behind.

Her thoughts drifted to the sacrifices of the past few years— long hours, personal loss, and a relentless drive that had strained every part of her life. She glanced at the glowing panel, a reflection of her pursuit. This was it, the culmination of decades of work, and yet, the hollow ache of what it had cost her remained. She'd lost Sarah, her daughter, and though this project was a way to honor her memory, it had also widened the chasm between her and Henry.Taking a deep breath, she turned toward the main lab, where Henry was reconnecting QUEST 0.9 into its storage bank.

"Henry," she called, her voice tinged with anticipation, "I think it's time."

Henry walked over,tall, broad-shouldered despite his years, with silvered hair that he kept neatly combed back. Wiping his hands on a lint-free cloth. He placed a reassuring hand on her shoulder, glancing at the camera. "I think we've done it, Amber. Decades of research and innovation have led us to this point. Once QUEST 1.0 is assembled, we're ready."

Amber turned her chair to face him. "Henry, I know I've been... difficult these last few years. Since Sarah - ." Her voice

4

faltered.

Henry squeezed her shoulder gently. "Amber, I know. I know what Sarah meant to you, to us. Your drive and focus were always what drew me to you, even back then. I haven't always been the partner you needed, but I'm still here."

He searched her face for a flicker of the woman he married – the fierce, compassionate visionary who had built Quantum Biotech Solutions with him. She was still there, beneath layers of grief and ambition, and it was that belief that kept him grounded.

The sound of the lab door sliding open interrupted them. Hugo Victor, tall and impeccably dressed, strode in, his polished British accent cutting through the sterile air.

"Another successful transfer, team!" He clapped his hands lightly, a calculated display of enthusiasm. "I'll be meeting with Spectrum tomorrow. News of this success will bolster their interest in joining forces with us."

Henry's expression darkened. "Hugo, Spectrum's involvement in the AI program is as far as I'm willing to go. No one outside the QUEST team can know how far we've come."

Hugo nodded, his diplomatic smile unfaltering. "Of course, Henry. But their contributions have been invaluable. The hardware advancements alone have accelerated our timeline significantly."

Amber interjected, "Henry, Hugo has a point. Spectrum's resources could bring QUEST to market faster. We've always managed partnerships carefully, and this could be no different."

Henry shook his head. "No. Our focus stays internal. Let's celebrate tonight and brief the team tomorrow. We're at a pivotal stage, and I won't risk it."

Amber exchanged a glance with Hugo, her expression un-readable. Over the past decade, she and Henry had assembled a team of unparalleled talent, drawing from disciplines as diverse as material engineering, quantum computing, neuroscience, and physics. They'd built technologies that defied imagination, each breakthrough paving the way for the next. It had been a delicate balance of vision and pragmatism, and every decision carried weight.

As the lab quietened for the evening, Amber lingered near the cleanroom's observation panel. She watched Henry and Hugo leave, their conversation trailing off into the hallway. Alone with her thoughts, she replayed Hugo's words in her mind. Spectrum's interest was no surprise, but Henry's reluctance gnawed at her. She trusted him implicitly, but the future of QUEST required calculated risks.

Amber turned back to the workstation, her reflection in the black screen catching her off guard. For a moment, she saw not the driven scientist, but a woman weighed down by loss and ambition. She shook the thought away and began drafting her next log entry.

"The future isn't a fixed point," she murmured to herself. "It's something we shape."

2

Chapter 2: Shifting Tides

Amber placed her book on the nightstand and pressed the button to raise the blinds. As the fabric receded into the ceiling recess, the first morning rays illuminated the bedroom. From her vantage point, the city stretched before her, a sea of glass towers catching the warm light. Even after decades of living here, the beauty of the skyline never ceased to amaze her. She closed her eyes and inhaled deeply, centering herself in the quiet stillness of dawn.

Moments like this reminded her why she pursued her work with such fervor. Time - more time to enjoy the world, to explore ideas, to be with the people she loved. This quest for time had driven her for decades, shaping every decision and every sacrifice. She knew today would be pivotal, a step closer to achieving her life's ambition. Yet, the enormity of the task ahead settled heavily in her chest.

Amber swung her legs over the edge of the bed, her feet sinking into the plush woollen carpet. "Sixty-two years," she murmured to the empty room. "So much done, so much more to do."

She pulled on her robe and padded into the kitchen, turning on the espresso machine. The hum of the grinder filled the air as she scooped fresh beans into the hopper. The aroma of coffee mingled with the faint metallic tang of the city air streaming through the open window. She pulled two espresso cups from the drawer just as she heard the front door open.

Henry entered, his face flushed from his morning run. He wore a damp singlet and shorts, his silver-streaked hair matted with sweat. Despite his seventy-odd years, he moved with a youthful energy, his military discipline still evident in his posture and stride.

"Morning, Ambs," he said, wiping his brow with a towel.

"Morning, mister. Coffee now or after your shower?" she asked, holding up the cups.

"After the shower. I've got a message from Hugo – he's got a presentation lined up before we start today. Hugo and his driver will pick us all up at 8:30."

Amber nodded, placing the cups back on the counter. "Must be about that new polymer casing. His brief last week mentioned promising results in impact resistance. Probably pitching it to Spectrum, I assume?"

Henry's expression soured. "Spectrum again? I wish we could distance ourselves from them."

"I understand your reservations, Henry, but they've been instrumental in getting us this far. Cutting ties now would set us back years."

"Maybe. But I don't trust their intentions," Henry replied, his voice firm. "We'll keep this partnership strictly professional – no deeper entanglements."

At 8:30 sharp, the company Mercedes pulled up in front of their building. Amber, Henry, and Hugo climbed into the sleek, black van, its leather interior cool against the warmth of the morning. The conversation flowed easily at first, touching on Hugo's team's recent progress.

"Henry, I think you'll be pleased with today's presentation," Hugo said, tapping away on his tablet. "The nanocomposite casing is performing beyond expectations - durable, lightweight, and versatile."

"Good. But don't let Spectrum dictate terms on this one," Henry warned.

Hugo gave a measured nod. "Noted."

The van pulled into the QBS Headquarters at Hudson Yards, a gleaming tower of steel and glass that housed their operations. Inside, the trio passed through security and headed directly to the executive boardroom, where Hugo's materials engineering team was already assembled.

The presentation was crisp and professional. Hugo outlined the advancements in polymer nanocomposites, emphasizing their potential applications in military and industrial sectors. The slides showcased data from rigorous stress tests, comparing the new material to conventional alternatives.

"This is impressive," Henry said, examining a sample of the material. "It's robust enough to survive almost anything. We'll need to strategise its rollout carefully."

"This kind of innovation reinforces our position at the forefront of materials science. Let's prioritise patent applications and explore partnerships beyond Spectrum," Amber added.

Hugo's team distributed samples - personalised phone cases - to the executives. Amber turned hers over in her hand, noting the lightweight feel and sleek design. It was a tangible reminder of their team's ingenuity and the potential for widespread application.

As the meeting wrapped up, Amber placed a hand on Hugo's arm. "Outstanding work. Let's regroup after the Spectrum meeting to plan our next steps."

Hugo gave a small smile. "Of course, Amber."

In the lab later that afternoon, the trio stood before the 3D printers assembling the components of QUEST 1.0. Amber leaned closer to the glass, her breath fogging the surface slightly. Inside, the machines worked with precise efficiency, constructing layer-by-layer the synthetic brain that represented decades of research.

"Everything has led to this moment," Amber whispered, her voice filled with awe. "Years of breakthroughs, sacrifices, and determination. This is it."

Henry placed a hand on her shoulder, a rare gesture of quiet support. "Let's make it count."

As the machines continued their work, the hum of progress filled the room, echoing the quiet determination of the team. The future was taking shape, one layer at a time.

3

Chapter 3: Into the Unknown

4:00 PM, QBS QUEST Lab

The sprawling, state-of-the-art facility occupied the entirety of the sixth floor, designed to accommodate every stage of the consciousness transfer process. The lab was meticulously divided into specialized zones, each a masterpiece of modern engineering. The controlled hum of high-precision equipment resonated through the air, punctuated by the faint beeping of diagnostic monitors. Adjustable LED lighting bathed the room in a sterile, shadowless glow, ensuring optimal focus in critical areas. Walls of frosted glass and polished stainless steel reflected the soft light, giving the space a futuristic, yet grounded, aura.

Ergonomically designed workstations and touch-interactive control panels lined the walls, while banks of servers emitted a quiet, rhythmic whir. In one corner, a holographic display projected the intricate neural map of QUEST 1.0, its luminescent lines pulsating like a living organism. It was a facility built not just for science, but for precision and progress.

Amber stood on the other side of the glass wall, dressed in a hospital gown. She moved carefully, aware of the weight of the moment. Henry, in the adjacent control room, watched her through the glass, his expression a mixture of pride and apprehension. His voice crackled over the intercom.

"You've been ready for this a long time, haven't you, Ambs?"

Amber smiled faintly, her fingers brushing against the IV stand. "Originally, I thought we'd unlock something genetic - a way to extend life at the molecular level. If you'd asked me in 1979 whether we could transfer consciousness into a synthetic brain, I'd have laughed."

Henry chuckled. "Our path has changed a few times, hasn't it? Pharmaceuticals, genetics, digital mapping... Now we're building entirely new materials just to keep up with our science."

Amber's gaze drifted toward the ceiling as the anaesthetist adjusted the IV. Her mind wandered to Sarah. It had been Sarah's idea to explore alternative ways of housing consciousness, her sharp intellect pushing their theoretical models forward. Even after Sarah's illness became evident, she'd worked tirelessly, her passion undimmed by her failing body. Losing her daughter had left a void that no breakthrough could fill, but it also fueled Amber's determination. This was for Sarah. It always had been.

"Henry, this is for Sarah," Amber said softly, her voice steady. "If we succeed tonight, no one will ever have to lose a loved one again."

Henry nodded, his throat tightening as he keyed the intercom. He didn't trust himself to speak. Hugo, standing beside him, adjusted his tie and leaned toward the mic. "Amber, I know you designed this process, but let's run through it verbally. Stage one: the compound is introduced intravenously to relax your body and sedate most muscle movements. Life support systems will stabilize your vitals while your brain shifts into beta waves. At that point, you'll need to focus your consciousness on the void - the nothingness around you. When we detect theta waves, stage two will commence, introducing the second compound. You'll remain in this state for approximately six hours while we map your neural structure onto QUEST."

Amber met Hugo's gaze through the glass. "How long until QUEST is ready?"

"Assembly is complete. AI structure analysis and system purification will be done in fifteen minutes," Henry replied. His voice carried a note of optimism he didn't entirely feel. "You'll be dancing in the lounge room by this time tomorrow, Ambs."

The anaesthetist finished loading the compounds into the automated delivery system. The computerised monitors displayed Amber's vitals in clean, precise lines. Everything was ready.

Henry and Hugo thanked the anaesthetists, who exited the room, leaving the process entirely in their hands. In the control room, the hum of electronics surrounded them. The monitors displayed a cascade of data - heart rate, brain activity, compound absorption rates - each parameter a testament to their meticulous planning.

"OK, Amber," Henry said, his voice steady through the intercom. "Are you ready to proceed?"

Amber's lips curved into a faint smile. "Ready as I'll ever

be."

As the first compound entered her bloodstream, Amber closed her eyes, her breathing slowing. Henry watched the monitor as her brainwaves transitioned from alpha to beta. The sight filled him with a mix of awe and dread. This was uncharted territory. They had mapped countless animal brains, but this was the first human attempt.

Hugo's attention was fixed on the neural data stream. "Beta waves detected. Theta shouldn't be far behind."

The minutes dragged, each one stretching into eternity. Henry's mind raced with possibilities: What if something went wrong? What if the synthetic brain rejected the data? What if...

"Theta waves detected," Hugo announced, breaking the silence. "Stage two commencing."

The second compound flowed into Amber's veins, and her vitals stabilised. The qubit processors began their work, mapping her neural structure with unparalleled precision. QUEST 1.0, housed in its assembly booth, hummed to life as terabytes of data streamed into its synthetic neural network. The room filled with the sound of progress, a quiet symphony of machines working toward a singular goal.

Henry leaned back, exhaling deeply. "Now we wait."

Hugo nodded, his gaze still fixed on the monitors. "Six hours to map, one hour to audit. By dawn, we'll know."

Henry's eyes flicked to the assembly booth where QUEST 1.0 stood, its sleek surface gleaming under the lab's lights. It represented decades of dreams, sacrifices, and resilience. He glanced at the screen displaying Amber's neural map, its complexity both beautiful and terrifying. This wasn't just a scientific achievement; it was a testament to everything they had built together.

As the hours stretched on, the hum of the machines became a soothing rhythm. Yet, beneath the surface, an undercurrent of tension lingered. This was their moment - the culmination of everything. And it was just the beginning.

4

Chapter 4: Fractured Loyalties

As the procedure began, Amber felt the first compound enter her arm. The cool liquid took only a second to travel up her arm and reach her shoulder. She closed her eyes and concentrated on her breath, slipping into a state of profound tranquility. The world around her faded away, replaced by a sense of weightlessness and serenity that enveloped her. It was as if she was floating in a sea of pure consciousness, untethered by the constraints of time and space. There was nothing - no light, no sound, no one. Yet she felt safe.

Completely unaware of the passage of time, Amber remained in this ethereal state for hours. Aided by a cocktail of pharmacological aids, her consciousness hung suspended in the void as QUEST 1.0's brain hummed with life in the other room.

"Henry, Amber is well into the theta brainwave state, and all readouts look very positive. The qubit processors show large volumes of data being transferred to QUEST," Hugo reported.

"Mostly looks good, mate, but my concern is this structural mapping gap that we got a couple hours in," Henry said, passing Hugo a tablet with a timeline diagnosis displayed on the screen.

"That happened on QUEST 0.8, but data integrity was confirmed once the process was complete."

"I know, Hugo. But will this cause issues for the contained consciousness when accessing the stored data?"

"There's no real way to say. This is the first time we're using a consciousness that might actually be able to tell us, once it's finished. Theoretically, after the transfer, we should be able to go back in and add quantum neural paths to those segments."

Henry turned to look at his wife lying in the theater. A quiet moment passed.

"I know, as scientists and pioneers, we need to reach for the stars. Every leap in science and technology has brought ethical questions throughout history. I just never dreamed I'd be on the leading edge. This is definitely Amber's dream."

Hugo stood. "Too true, old chap. She is one determined woman. I feel like her gravity pulls us along. We have a big night ahead, I'll head downstairs and grab us some coffee. We'll need our energy - we're part of something exciting and daunting."

"Thanks, Hugo. I might pop next door and grab one of the laptops. I want to run an AI model to see how the quantum neural paths might look if there's a storage gap in QUEST 1.0."

"Good shout. I'll meet you back here in 10 minutes."

Henry swiped his access card and placed his hand on the biometric reader to enter the Quantum Computing Lab. The light flicked on as he entered, and he strolled to the laptop bank. At the hub terminal, he entered the laptop number he wanted and requested the AI interface to load it with a model of the current QUEST 1.0 transfer and any potential storage gaps. After a few interactions with the AI prompts, Henry finally hit "confirm" to load the model onto the laptop. Satisfied with the results, he checked his watch – he'd been in the Quantum Computing Lab for just over 10 minutes.

Henry looked at his Bulova. "Hugo will be back any minute," he said to himself

The Quantum Computing Lab shared a wall with the transfer theater, which was sandwiched between it and the Quantum Server Room. Both had large observation windows facing the theater. As Henry unplugged the loaded laptop, he turned to look at Amber, lying still on the bed. Although he couldn't quite see into the control room clearly due to the reflection on the glass, he saw the light from the control room's sliding door.

"There he is – right on time with my caffeine hit."

Henry strolled back to the control room, the laptop held out in front of him. He had opened it and already started scrolling through with one hand on the interface for the AI model he had just loaded.

As he reached the control room door, he knocked with his free hand, announcing to Hugo that he had a virtual model ready. The door slid open, and Henry stepped into the dimly lit space, still looking at his laptop screen.

"Hugo, mate, I will need your help with this. You are a whiz with these models."

Still clicking away, Henry lowered the screen when Hugo didn't reply. His eyes took a few seconds to adjust to the shadows of the room. "Who the fuck are you?!"

Henry was staring into the small round muzzle of a sup-pressed handgun, followed by a pair of cold, dark eyes nestled in a bizarre-looking ski mask. The material of the figure's clothes was also oddly textured and dark, seeming to absorb all light. Henry saw the figure tighten his grip on the pistol, ever so slightly. His instinct exploded into action, throwing the laptop at his assailant. The shrouded figure was not expecting this 72-year-old scientist to move so quickly. The laptop connected with the intruder's shoulder, turning him slightly. With the impact, a loud sound rang out in the control room, a muffled report of a suppressed firearm. Henry felt a fierce impact above his collarbone. The black-clad figure spared no moment and stepped forward towards Henry, aiming a second round directly into his heart. The impact sent Henry tripping backward, smashing the back of his head on a monitor benchtop as he fell. Instant blackness.

As Compound 1 helped withdraw Amber from her body, the experience was almost mystical. The sensation was akin to gliding through an endless expanse, where the boundaries of self began to blur. Over the years of her research and pharmaceutical development, she had experienced this before. But the first time she ever experienced something mystical was in her mid-20s. She was experimenting with trance states, meditation, and psychedelics. She had even been able to get into a similar state by sitting quietly in the dark, concentrating on her breathing, slowly releasing physical awareness and sliding deeper into her subconscious. It was these experiences that made her explore the physiological side of these mystical practices and later develop reliable, consistent drugs that could do the same thing.

It was like floating in complete blackness, with an awareness that this blackness extended infinitely in every direction. It felt familiar and safe, a sensation of wholeness and connectedness. Thought was still possible, and the urge was to go deeper into this black, invisible field.

A realisation came over Amber while her consciousness floated in the endless void of the quantum field – the field that holds all matter together. The field that connects everything together. She had always imagined this place deep within her own subconscious, but this time it seemed clear that the subconscious was actually a doorway to something else. Just as this thought formed, another feeling swept through and over her awareness – a feeling of a mirror, a feeling of another, right there with her. It felt like love; it felt like an embrace from another presence. She could also feel that it was aware of her and that it felt the same for her. She was dual...and then there was only her again. The other vanished.

Ringing. No, not ringing; it was more like a constant high-pitched tone in his head. Pain, aching pain, seared the back of his head, his shoulder, and his chest. He could feel warmth on his face. Henry realized he was lying face down in his own blood – that old familiar smell, the iron taste in his mouth. He could feel the hard medical laminate floor under his cheek. Slowly he tried to move. Breathing hurt. Every movement was agonising. Propping himself up against the wall, he lifted his hand to his collarbone. About an inch above it, he felt a burning hole seeping blood. Thankfully, the bone still felt intact; luckily, the round must not have severed any major arteries either. He dropped his hand to his chest, wincing with pain, but confused. He felt something hard on his chest. His fingers slipped underneath his blood-soaked lab coat and found a buckled mobile phone. He yanked it out of his breast pocket. "The bloody nanocomposite phone case," Henry thought to himself.

There was no one else in the room now, but his hearing was coming back. The ringing was still there, but he could hear muffled talking from the hallway.

Henry realized he was listening to Hugo from outside the control room.

"...didn't need to unplug her. None of this was part of the deal."

A sharp, hot surge prickled Henry from his sternum to his fingertips as he heard these words. And then he realized what the ringing was; it wasn't his ears at all - it was Amber's vitals! Adrenaline surged through his aching body, instantly pushing down the pain. Henry lifted himself up to the observation window and looked at his motionless wife. The vitals screen in the control room was scrolling a flatline...with a countdown underneath it. Seconds ticking away, adding to the total - 25.07, 25.08, 25.09.... She had been flatlining for 25 minutes. He must have been unconscious at least that long.

Anger, rage, vengeance - a pulse of energy leapt into Henry and then a strong sense of hope - QUEST 1.0 could have his wife's consciousness on it.

Henry partially heard a quieter voice too, speaking English but with an accent, maybe Russian.

"...has to look like this...a murder...where is QUEST?"

"...QUEST is in the next room. I put it in a travel case. You can't just take Quest 1.0 if you want the whole project. You will also need the two server blocks. All Quest project data is stored on these two blocks - one on this level and a backup in the basement. The whole system is air-gapped from the outside world."

"...give me his key card and the travel case. I will go to the basement...and you get the server block from here...in the basement, then...meet at the car in the lane way. Here, take this.."

Something clicked in Henry; a coolness overcame him. He understood what was happening. He stood against the wall, listening intently. Hugo was speaking to the person who shot him, giving directions. Hugo sounded extremely angry, a tightness up in his throat. "I'll slit that throat, you traitorous fucking snake," Henry whispered to himself.

He could hear footsteps down the hall and another door open-ing, then, in the other direction, footsteps heading towards the elevator lobby. Ducking down below window level, Henry slid across the control room floor and peeked above the sill. He could just make out Hugo in the quantum-server room on the opposite side of the theatre. It looked like he was already wheeling a small trolley out of the server dock to the door.

If he had the QUEST server block on the trolley, it would be a black rectangular box with a quick-release lever on the front side and rows of fibre-optic docks on the rear. Only the size of a shoebox but over 20 kg in weight. The solid-state server blocks were actually a very early prototype for QUEST; although able to store immense amounts of data, their construction was too large and the crystal storage cells were too fragile for use in a synthetic brain application like QUEST. Completely suitable for use as servers that would be stationary.

Henry decided to wait until Hugo was out in the lobby and then make a move. He slid his ruined lab coat off and got ready to sneak out of the control room. He had to get that travel case with QUEST back. Amber could still be on there.

Just as Hugo wheeled past the control room door, Henry poised himself for the exit, reaching for his key card. His card was missing; usually clipped to a lanyard on his waist, it had been removed while he was unconscious. Hugo must have given it to the intruder, who would need it down in the basement to access the backup server room. The key card alone wouldn't gain access though; they would need a biometric read also...like a bloody palm print. Henry looked at his palms, coated in his own blood, which was now dry and crusty. They could potentially have his palm print swabbed to lay on the scanner in the basement. Henry needed to get out of the control room; luckily, being on the secure side of the door, he could use the manual release for the door operation. The delay meant Henry missed his chance; he could hear the elevator chime in the lobby. Hugo must have already entered his floor selection and called the elevator on the access pad.

Sliding the control room door back just enough to squeeze out, he was careful to step quietly with his bloody Oxfords, silently leaving crimson footprints as he padded down the corridor to the lobby corner. Henry peeked around the corner to see Hugo waiting at the elevator doors. His heart sank as he saw two more motionless bodies in lab coats. His anaesthetists laid face up on the lobby floor, also with dark burgundy stains on their coats and thick puddles forming under their torsos.

As the elevator arrived, it chimed and the doors began to open. This was his chance. Hugo started to push the server trolley into the lift. Henry sprang around the corner, crossed the lobby in a few quick strides pushing all his momentum into a shoulder charge. Hugo heard the closest steps and turned to see a furious, bloodied Henry hurtling towards him, only just managing to raise his elbow and shoulder, bracing for impact as Henry crashed into him. The two men burst into

23

the elevator, toppled over the trolley and slammed in a tangled mess on the floor. Both stunned, tying to get on their feet, the elevator chimed again and the door closed. Hugo, the much younger, less injured man was on his feet a second before Henry. Astonished to see him alive but recognising the situation, Hugo wound up his right arm for a big hey-maker. Not a trained fighter, telegraphing the movement with plenty of time for Henry to catch his arm. Hugo, panicking, threw his free arm at Henry's face. Easily catching this one too, Henry held both the younger man's arms, wrapped tightly under his. Looking face to face, Henry pushed his whole-body forwards, pummelling Hugo into the wall of the elevator and held him there for a second. Long enough for Hugo the look into Henry's cold stare.

"You sold us out, you fucking drop-kick"

"You don't understand, not half of it. We didn't want it to go this way, Henry!"

"You traitorous fucking lizard, you just aided the murder of my wife"

Before Hugo could respond, Henry slammed his forehead into Hugo's nose, dropping him like a rag doll.

Hugo fell to the floor of the elevator with blood streaming from the mashed nose. Whimpering, Hugo clutched his hands to his face

"I didn't mean for this; I was told it was just the data they wanted!"

Henry kicked the English man sharply in the ribs making him double over and lay face down on the elevator floor.

"Let me guess, your Spectrum mates are behind this?! Not many people would send a goon with signature-reducing fatigues on. That tech shouldn't exist yet. We were the ones who produced the models for visual-magnetic-wave-disruption. How long have you been selling us out?!"

Hugo, gasping and pushing himself up to his elbows shouted back. "You have no idea! Spectrum has been with you since the beginning, before I even came to work for QBS! You don't really know how your relationship with Spectrum started!"

With this Henry reached down and grabbed Hugo's shoulder to turn him over. Pulling him round he was surprised to see a gun in his hand. With instant reflex, Henry tried to slap the pistol away. The Russian-made PL-15K pistol barked angrily as Henry's hand clipped Hugo in the forearm. Although the pistol clattered to the onyx floor of the elevator, Henry felt a sting in his upper arm and recoiled backwards. Hugo lunged urgently towards the fallen pistol, eager to re-arm himself. Henry kicked the server trolley into Hugo, the server block tumbled off and landed on his head. Hugo, still dazed from the heavy impact of the server block, Henry stepped over to him and with a vicious surge, picked up the block above his own head. He brought it down on Hugo again, and again, and again and again.

Henry realised he was completely out of breath. Only just comprehending what he did, the gruesome evidence of violence lay all around him. Chunks of data crystal and server components strewn across the elevator floor smeared with blood. His face speckled with Hugo's life-force. No longer able to stand and for the first time feeling his age, he sagged to the floor.

The elevator chimed once more, jarring Henry out of his daze. He remembered – he must get Amber back. He checked his upper left arm, only a grazing wound on the inside of his arm. Snatching up the Russian pistol, he steadied himself and went to make his way to the building's rear alley.

Rounding the service corridor, he could see another body

halfway through a doorway, propping open the door itself. It was a QBS security guard.

Raising his firearm and stepping over the murdered man, he emerged into the alley. Henry saw the assailant loading what looked like the other server block and a new nanocomposite travel container into the passenger side of a black Range Rover before getting into the driver's seat.

Determining that QUEST 1.0 was most likely in the container, he rushed the vehicle. The intruder saw Henry coming, slamming his foot onto the accelerator.

Henry fired three rounds from the pistol, exploding the passenger window into a shower of safety glass. The driver, trying to avoid the incoming fire, ducked and subsequently yanked the steering wheel of the large SUV. Smashing into a dumpster, it was the crucial moment Henry needed to leap onto the vehicle from the front passenger door and reach for the driver.

Grabbing onto the thick signature-reducing material of the intruder's fatigues, he could see another silenced pistol knocked to the floor by the impact with the dumpster. The driver, fighting Henry off with one hand and steering with the other, accelerated, hurtling down the lane. Swinging the vehicle left and right, desperate to rid himself of the man half hanging out the passenger window. Still holding onto the fatigues with one hand, he was forced to release the pistol to pull himself into the cabin to avoid being cut in half by another incoming dumpster.

Inside the cabin of the luxury 4x4, a messy scuffle ensued. Short jabs and elbows rained down from both opponents, but the Russian was stronger and more skilled. Henry received a punch to his left ear, which disoriented him, followed by a heavy elbow to his nose and another to his temple. This brought more blackness.

Determined to get as much distance between him and the facility, the Russian operative kept his foot flat to the floor and soared through the Lincoln Tunnel, keen to get to a hidden rendezvous in the derelict district. With a quick glance at the injured man in the passenger seat, he noticed it looked as though Henry was dead. He remained slumped in the passenger seat, drawing shallow breaths. No real threat.

Suddenly, wind hit him in the face. The thwack of rotor blades and the view of thick jungle far below him. The chopper was heading into the setting sun, and its spinning rotors flashed light and shadow on Henry's face as he leaned against the sliding door of the helicopter. The rotors seemed to be slowing down, the flash of the sunlight almost winding backward. Pain and heaviness swamped his body; his head felt filled with lead and his cheekbone hurt. Henry realised his eyes were actually closed and that his face was leaning against something hard. The light of the sunset, broken by the spin of the rotors, was replaced with street lights passing overhead. Realisation flooded back: he was back in the Range Rover, with his head against the shattered passenger window pane. Not daring to show any movement, Henry began to gather his strength.

A burst of determination launched him at the driver. Trying to seize the steering wheel, Henry yanked down with all the strength he could muster. Pulling the car into the guard rail, the sudden collision sent their car careening through the barrier, hurtling through the darkness until it crashed into an abandoned building, its walls crumbling around them in a storm of destruction and debris.

The impact sent Henry hurtling through the windshield,

along with QUEST 1.0. Time slowed for him. He tumbled across concrete, bricks, and rubble, feeling things break inside him. His body stopped tumbling, but he saw the container continue to skitter past him in a landslide of rubble and glass. It slid across what appeared to be an abandoned factory floor - only to fall out of sight in a cloud of dust.

Henry did not know how much time had passed since he watched Quest fall into the drain. He still lay there, unable to turn his head away. His body was not responding. It didn't hurt, but he felt cold. He felt tired. He felt a heavy curtain being drawn across his vision. There was no resistance left in him – Henry let go.

As the dust settled and the echoes of the crash faded away, their fates were sealed in a violent crescendo of destruction. Fuel leaked onto the floor from the ruptured tank, sparks igniting the flammable liquid, engulfing the Range Rover. The flames wrapped around the SUV and its contents. The battered Russian and the last remaining evidence of the Quest project returned to ash in a gasoline-fueled incineration of twisted metal and smashed glass.

5

Chapter 5: Gathering Information

As Mia pounded the path through Central Park, she felt her phone vibrate in the hip pocket of her activewear. A quick glance at her smartwatch showed it was the office. She touched her earbuds to activate the call without breaking her stride.

"Yes?"

"Last night didn't go to plan. We need to start cleaning up. Be here by 0930."

The voice belonged to Lena Reinhardt, Director of Intelligence Operations at Spectrum, USA. Lena, an ex-CIA operative, was renowned for her meticulous attention to detail and unyielding drive to maintain Spectrum's dominance in the tech and intelligence sectors. A formidable figure, she was both feared and respected within the organization. Lena had been instrumental in forging critical relationships with the U.S. defense sector, leveraging Spectrum's cutting-edge technology to cement their influence.

"I'll be there," Mia replied, her voice calm and measured. She tapped her earbuds to end the call and veered onto a side path, cutting her morning run short.

Mia entered the Spectrum lobby, her open-toed heels clicking sharply on the polished concrete floor. She passed her Kors handbag through the X-ray scanner and swiped her ID card at the security turnstile before heading to the elevator.

When the elevator doors opened, Lena Reinhardt was already in the executive lobby, speaking briskly to her personal assistant. Without waiting, Lena waved Mia over and turned toward her office corridor. She swiped her access card at her office door and held it open for Mia.

"Take a seat, Carter. We need to be quick."

"Yes, ma'am," Mia said, pulling out the sleek, ergonomic chair from in front of Lena's imposing glass desk.

Lena wasted no time. "Last night's operation went to shit, but it won't be a complete loss if we act quickly. The picture we intended to paint should still hold. Our Russian asset did what he was supposed to and was terminated in a vehicle collision. It seems Mr. Spinks had more fight in him than we anticipated. Unfortunately, all digital records of the Quest project were destroyed before the rendezvous. We also lost one of our inside assets - Hugo."

Mia's expression remained neutral. "I see. So the Russian narrative will play out, but we're left empty-handed. Were all other objectives completed? Both Spinks eliminated?"

Lena nodded, her tone clipped. "Correct. The termination of Amber Spinks leaves a strategic opening for us. With Henry dead in the crash while trying to stop the 'Russian operative', our new model predicts a high probability of a merger with QBS. The remaining board members are susceptible to pressure. Once the merger is finalised, we'll have access to their prototypes and historical research to reverse-engineer the Quest system."

Mia leaned forward slightly. "And in the meantime?"

"We need to secure as much historical material as possible," Lena said, her voice sharp with urgency. "Henry's journals, their video logs - everything. Your job is to get your team into their lab and apartment to recover it. Any remaining research can be acquired during the merger process."

Mia nodded. "Understood. That will give us a head start on rebuilding Quest in the months ahead of the merger."

"Exactly," Lena said, standing and straightening the cuffs of her tailored blazer. "Let's get moving."

Mia quickly divided her team into two units. One group would handle the surgical break-in at Amber and Henry's apartment, while the other would infiltrate the lab using insider agents. Their objective: gather every scrap of remaining information on the Quest project.

The team assigned to the apartment had insider access to the building's security system, allowing them to overwrite the surveillance feeds with AI-generated footage. The operatives entered unnoticed, heading directly to a private office Mia had identified as their target. According to Lena, Henry had been a meticulous journal writer, recording decades of insights and observations. Every single journal was critical. The catastrophic loss of the Quest server blocks during the failed operation had left Spectrum scrambling to recover any semblance of the project. The journals, alongside family photos, letters, and even home security recordings, would form the foundation of their efforts to reconstruct Quest.

At the lab, Spectrum's insider agents coordinated with the second team. The operatives bypassed the lab's outer defenses and began combing through years of video logs, lab recordings, and team brainstorming sessions. While the Quest server blocks had contained the core data, these secondary materials offered valuable context and insights. Accidental recordings of off-the-cuff ideas, heated debates, and technical breakthroughs were all fair game.

As the hours ticked by, Mia oversaw the operation from Spectrum's intelligence hub, her sharp eyes scanning the feeds from both teams. The stakes were high, but Mia knew Lena's unrelenting drive would brook no excuses. Spectrum's future dominance hinged on their ability to rebuild Quest - piece by painstaking piece.

By dawn, the operatives had extracted terabytes of data, dozens of journals, and countless artifacts from the Spinks' personal and professional lives. Mia reviewed the initial reports with a sense of grim satisfaction. The failed operation had been a setback, but with the materials now in Spectrum's possession, the path forward was clear. They would rebuild Quest, not as a legacy of the Spinks' brilliance, but as a testament to Spectrum's unyielding control.

6

Chapter 6: Discovery

Roman lifted the hammer once again, heaving the steel sledge into the ancient brick wall. The thud of the impact echoed through the empty factory, and a shower of crumbling brick added to the pile of rubble at his feet. "One more hit should do it," he thought. Demand for his off-grid bio-mech surgery had increased over the past couple of years, and removing this wall would finally give him the extra floor space he wanted - a simple investment in his growing side hustle. Every inch meant more room for paying clients.

Once, Roman had been a rising star in the bio-tech industry, his skills coveted by the biggest corporations. Born amid the chaos of the corporate wars, he'd left a turbulent Russia behind for the apparent stability of the new East States of America (ESA). His talent had quickly secured him a position with one of the top bio-mech companies. Roman was a visionary, his promise limitless. But his ascent was cut short when an incident forced his hasty departure from the corporate world.

The official records only hinted at the truth, but those who knew Roman well understood what had happened. A combination of addiction, overconfidence, and relentless ambition pushed him past his limits. Enhancements to his own body gave him an edge - a bio-mech exoskeleton to steady his hands and synthetic neural boosts for focus - but his addiction to performance stimulants spiraled out of control. During one critical procedure, his modifications failed him, and a patient died. The patient had been a test subject with a unique, expensive implant, and the fallout was catastrophic. The company covered up the failure, but Roman's career was over.

Despite the disgrace, Roman left the corporate world without regret. He'd grown disillusioned with their hollow morality and saw more opportunity in the shadows of the underground bio-tech scene. Here, he built a name for himself, free from regulations and ethics boards. Nestled in the decaying industrial zone known as the Tangle, Roman's practice catered to those who valued discretion and had the credits to pay.

With the wall finally down, Roman surveyed the expanded room, nodding at the added client space. He wheeled over the electric dolly and dumpster, filling it with bricks as the afternoon light waned. Outside, the Tangle buzzed with life. Vendors hawked their wares, repair shops hummed with machinery, and the aroma of makeshift eateries filled the air. It was chaotic and grimy, but to Roman, it was home.

After clearing the rubble, Roman grabbed his coffee and a pack of Nova Cigari from a vending machine outside. Sitting on an abandoned metal crate, he pulled his gloves off, exposing his hands. They were rough and worn, a testament to years of survival and hard work. His left forearm gleamed with polished metal, the bio-mech augmentation a blend of necessity and pride. Lighting a cigarette on the pack's ignition strip, he

35

leaned back, savoring the earthy taste of real tobacco. Synthetic alternatives had always tasted artificial to him, and this small indulgence was one of the few luxuries he allowed himself.

Propping his boots on a nearby pile of bricks, Roman let his mind wander. "Funny how things go around in circles," he muttered, exhaling smoke toward the factory's sawtooth roof. "Guess lung cancer's not much of a worry anymore." He stretched his feet out, and one of his boots landed with a hollow thud.

Curious, Roman set his coffee down and leaned over to inspect the sound. Brushing away dust, he uncovered the edges of a square recess in the concrete floor, perhaps an old drain. But as he dug further, his fingers grazed something solid. With growing excitement, he pried it free - a small, heavy container, about the size of a shoebox. The surface was made of high-tech, resilient material, and a faded QBS logo was stamped beneath an airtight latch.

"Well, well, what have we here?" Roman smirked, his interest piqued. The logo stirred faint memories of corporate whispers and old tech scandals. "Didn't think QBS stuff was still kicking around."

He ran his fingers over the latch, testing its seal. Whatever was inside, it had been buried deep for a reason. Roman's mind raced with possibilities: advanced tech, credits, leverage - perhaps even secrets that someone would pay dearly to recover.

Leaning back against the wall, Roman lit another Nova and stared at the container resting in the dust at his feet. Whatever this was, it was a relic of a world he thought he'd left behind. But in the Tangle, nothing stayed buried forever.

CHAPTER 6: DISCOVERY

7

Chapter 7: A Hopeful Experiment

Minimal regulation was just dandy for Roman and many other grey-market establishments. Cheap rent and less scrutiny. In New York, the outer areas were often nicknamed 'the Tangle' - a labyrinth of humanity and technology, business and pleasure; those who thrived and those who merely survived, those who lived and those who died. The Tangle was an ecosystem that nourished itself from the discarded opulence of the Corpo cities. Yet the corporate mainstream also relied on the Tangle. On the surface, there was open conflict between the two worlds, but underneath, a balance had been reached, and Roman felt deeply intertwined in it. He felt the pulse of Tangle life.

Roman went back inside his transportable prefab and stepped into the shower. The lukewarm water ran down his wiry frame, a mix of weariness and focus in his eyes. He was a man who bore the scars of his past - both literal and figurative - and carried the weight of his decisions with a quiet determination. Emerging clean, he toweled off and walked to his workbench. The QBS container sat there, an enigma waiting to be unraveled.

Adjusting the angle of his long-armed lamp, Roman directed its beam onto the mysterious box.

The container appeared to be constructed from a lightweight nanocomposite panel. For something that had been buried under a pile of rubble, it barely looked marked. Hesitating for a second, Roman's fingers hovered over the clasped airtight mechanism. His pulse quickened with curious excitement. He lifted the clasps, and the top of the container hissed open. Nestled in anti-vibration foam molding was an antiquated cerebral unit - or, as the Tangle often referred to it, a synth-brain.

The synth-brain was not as streamlined as the current ware Roman was familiar with, but something about it felt familiar. If designed for a human skull, it would occupy most of the frontal lobe. Its construction was unlike anything he'd seen before: surfaces shimmered with an iridescent hue, like bismuth crystals growing from synthetic panels. Erratic geometric patterns ran across parts of it, and small diode indicators sat dormant beside a unique fiber-optic connection point. There were no silicon chips or conventional electronics anywhere on it.

Roman woke his desktop terminal with the tap of a worn orange button set into the top of his keypad. Grabbing a hand-held 3D scanner, he methodically stroked a virtual beam across the synth-brain, watching as a 3D representation emerged on his monitor. Once the scan was complete, he activated his AI assistant to analyze the materials and suggest a diagnostic procedure to better understand how it worked. As his computer began its virtual deconstruction, Roman sat back in his creaking chair and lit another Nova Cigari.

The smoke curled lazily around his fingers as he watched

the progress bar inch forward. Thirty seconds later, his screen displayed a brief analysis:

- *Digital storage unit*
- *QBS logo on optic fiber ports – click here to display search results on "QBS"*
- *Age estimate: 100+ years*
- *Alloys – click here to display*
- *Unique materials – click here to display*
- *Assembly: molecular printing*
- *Power requirements: none*

Roman coughed as he read the last line. Blinking, he read it again. Still coughing on a lungful of South American smoke, he asked his terminal in his accented English, "What do you mean, no power?"

The terminal's text flickered briefly before responding in green text, as if it, too, was surprised:

Internal energy signal detected – unquantifiable capacity. No additional/external power requirements.

"What the fuck?!" Roman blurted, leaning back in his chair and putting his hands behind his head. Swiveling around, he gazed out his small window into the darkening factory. Pathways through the crowded transportable units were illuminated with hanging café lights and neon signs. The local residents were conducting their nightly business, their movements framed by a tangled overhead mess of fiber-optic cables, homemade satellite dishes, and pirate broadcasts. This was the Tangle – a chaotic, vibrant world that Roman now called home.

His stomach rumbled audibly, interrupting his thoughts.

Scratching his greying, bearded chin, Roman stood up. His body reminded him that the day's exertion had been fueled only by coffee and tobacco. "Food and thinking go together," he muttered. Looking back at his terminal, he issued a command: "Load QBS results onto my ComTab. I'll review it while I eat."

The main thoroughfare of the Tangle led Roman toward the old docks, where food barges brought goods and produce to the community. His favorite noodle spot, run by Danny, a third-generation Chinese chef, was set up on a concrete barge. The modular kitchen and bar, sheltered under a corrugated iron roof, served handmade noodles in Szechuan-style broth. The vat-grown meat was seasoned so well it didn't matter that it wasn't real, and they served Carlsberg in glass bottles - a rare treat.

Sitting at the bar, Roman slurped his spicy noodles as his ComTab read information directly into his auditory nerve. The history of QBS, or Quantum BioTech Solutions, unfolded in his mind. The company had begun in the 20th century, pioneering pharmaceuticals before branching into other areas of science. Their published papers laid the foundation for many of the modern technologies Roman worked with daily. But things had taken a dark turn: three of its leading directors were killed in a corporate espionage incident. Rumors tied the attack to a Russian competitor, though no definitive proof ever surfaced.

"Of course, leave it to us Russians to botch things up," Roman muttered with a chuckle, raising an eyebrow at the absurdity. The ComTab continued, detailing how Spectrum had stepped in to 'help' QBS during its crisis, eventually absorbing the smaller company. "And there we have it," Roman thought, "Spectrum's been swallowing companies ever since."

41

He leaned back, swirling the last of his noodles in the broth as the story trickled into his auditory nerve. The whole thing reeked of corporate sabotage, yet something didn't sit right. It felt... orchestrated. Too clean.

Roman slid off his stool and asked Danny for another Carlsberg for the road. He slid his payment bracelet across the reader embedded in the benchtop, watching the small holographic display flicker to life as it scanned the transaction. The screen lit up green with a quiet beep, confirming payment.

Nodding to Danny, Roman turned around to head in the direction of his prefab.

Back at his prefab, Roman locked the door and returned to his desk. The QBS device gleamed under the lamp, its enigmatic surfaces whispering secrets he was desperate to uncover. Picking it up, he turned it over in his hands. The top surface shimmered like a mineral, while the bottom resembled ancient circuitry pressed into charcoal-grey material. A fiber-optic connection port gleamed faintly - familiar yet alien.

Roman rummaged through his odds-and-ends box, finally pulling out a cable that seemed compatible. After a few adjustments with his needle-nose pliers, the cable clicked into place. Triumph flickered through him as his terminal came to life, running diagnostics on the device.

Hakisaka Terminal Assessment of Unknown Storage Device:

- *Hardware architecture: unknown - digital flush, undetermined capacity.*
- *Program language: unknown.*
- *Data packet sent and retrieved: no corruption.*

- *Assumed quantum computing power and entanglement theory processing realised.*

Roman's jaw tightened as he read the summary. Self-charging, quantum-level storage... it was more advanced than anything he'd ever seen. "How the hell did QBS manage this?" he muttered. Theories buzzed in his mind, but none seemed sufficient. This wasn't just a relic - it was a glimpse into a future long buried.

As the night wore on, Roman's thoughts churned with possibilities. The synth-brain sat silently on his desk, its mysteries pressing against his curiosity. Whatever it was, Roman knew one thing for certain: this discovery would change everything - for better or worse.

Roman stretched his arms, his chair creaking under his weight as he leaned back. His mind raced with the implications of what he had uncovered. This wasn't just some forgotten prototype - it was a Pandora's box. Yet, his excitement was tempered by caution. The Tangle wasn't the kind of place where secrets stayed hidden, and the last thing he needed was corporate goons sniffing around.

Pulling his chair closer, he typed a command into the terminal: *Initiate deeper analysis - focus on data signatures.* The progress bar crept forward, and Roman used the brief respite to brew a fresh pot of coffee. The scent of the bitter liquid filled his prefab, grounding him in the present.

The terminal dinged softly, and Roman nearly spilled his coffee rushing back to his desk.

Data Signatures Identified: Encrypted Data Present - Partial Reconstruction Possible.

Roman's eyes widened. "Encrypted data? After a century?

You've got to be kidding me," he muttered. He tapped a few more keys, instructing the system to reconstruct what it could. If this thing held information from the time of QBS, it might shed light on what happened to the company - or even why this synth-brain existed.

As the terminal worked, Roman paced the room, his mind flitting between the possibilities. The Corpo world wouldn't want something like this out in the open. If Spectrum had their fingers in QBS's pie, this device might hold secrets they'd buried long ago. Secrets worth killing for.

A sudden series of sharp knocks on the prefab's metal door snapped Roman out of his thoughts. His heart rate spiked. No one visited at this hour unless it was urgent - or trouble. Grabbing his Nova Cigari pack from the desk, he palmed the lighter concealed within and moved cautiously to the door.

"Who is it?" he barked, keeping his voice firm.

"It's Derik," came the muffled reply, a mix of urgency and relief in his tone. "Doc, we've got a situation."

Roman sighed and opened the door. Derik stood there, his face pale, sweat dripping down his temple. Behind him was an old-fashioned wheelchair with a slumped, bloodied figure barely clinging to life.

"Shit," Roman muttered, motioning them inside. "What the hell happened?"

Derik wheeled the chair in, his voice trembling. "Explosion. Some kind of firefight. Rod... he got hit in the head. It's bad, Roman. His ComTab - it's leaking brain fluid. You've got to help him."

Roman's gut twisted as he took in the scene. The man in the chair - Rod - looked like he'd been through hell. Blood streaked his face, pooling in the folds of his jacket. The fractured ComTab embedded in his skull was a grotesque sight, clear cerebral fluid trickling from the shattered edges.

"Put him on the table," Roman ordered, already moving to gather his tools. His hands, steady from years of practice, moved with precision, but his mind raced. The damage was catastrophic. Removing the ComTab wasn't an option - it would collapse the brain entirely. But leaving it as it was meant certain death.

As Roman worked, Derik paced nervously, rambling about the explosion. "It wasn't supposed to happen. We were just moving through when - "

"Quiet," Roman snapped, his focus unbroken. The room fell silent except for the hum of the life-support systems as they kicked in.

Derik was a wiry young man in his early twenties, his frame a mix of lean muscle and nervous energy. His olive-toned skin was faintly smudged with grease, a telltale sign of someone who worked with his hands more often than not. His black hair was cut short, uneven in places, as though he'd done it himself in front of a cracked mirror. He had sharp cheekbones and dark eyes that darted around, constantly scanning his surroundings, as if trouble lurked in every shadow.

He wore a patched-up utility jacket that had seen better days, its faded fabric bearing the logos of long-defunct companies. Underneath, a grimy T-shirt clung to him, the sweat and grime of the Tangle's streets adding to its wear. His boots, scuffed and mismatched, hinted at a life spent navigating uneven terrain and dodging trouble.

Though his outward appearance screamed scrapper, his hands told another story. Beneath the grime, they were steady and precise, the hands of someone who'd spent years fine-tuning machines and tweaking sensitive components. His voice carried the weight of someone older, edged with desperation and the faintest trace of hope, a contradiction to his restless demeanor.

Hours later, Roman stepped back, his hands trembling from fatigue. The ComTab was patched, the leaks stemmed, and Rod's vitals were stable -for now. But the damage was done. Scans confirmed that Rod's frontal lobe was beyond repair, the neural pathways dark. His body lived, but his mind... Roman shook his head. This wasn't life -it was a husk.

Roman turned to Derik, who sat slumped in a chair, his head in his hands. "Derik, I've done what I can. His body's stable, but his mind..." Roman hesitated, choosing his words carefully. "It's gone. All I'm doing is keeping the lights on."

Derik looked up, his eyes red. "There's nothing else you can do?"

Roman considered his next words. "There's one slim chance," he said, his voice low. "His ComTab's storage chip might still be intact. I've seen cases where memories - fragments of a person - can be extracted. It's not perfect, and it's not really them, but it's... something."

Derik's expression shifted to a fragile mix of hope and dread. "If there's a chance... we have to try. The people I work for... they'll want to know."

Roman stiffened. "The people you work for?" He stepped closer, his eyes narrowing. "You've been holding out on me, Derik. Rod's not just some guy, is he?"

Derik hesitated, then sighed. "He's... important. I can't say more, but there are people who'll want him alive - and people who'll do anything to keep him dead."

Roman's gaze shifted to the QBS device on his desk. The thought struck him like a lightning bolt. "Call your people," he said, his voice firm. "But let them know this: I'm not a charity. They pay in Lava Bucks. And whatever happens next, expect the unexpected."

Roman leaned back in his chair, letting a trail of smoke curl lazily from his Nova Cigari. The mention of 'Lava Bucks' tugged at the edges of his memory. For most, Lava Bucks were little more than whispers of a bygone era, a relic of an untraceable, tangible currency. But Roman? He knew better. They weren't just stories; they were history woven into the fabric of the underground.

Lava Bucks didn't emerge in boardrooms or corporate labs but from the chaos of a world grasping for control. Their origin was steeped in rebellion, birthed from necessity. As Roman stared at the synth-brain on his workbench, its shimmering surface catching the dim light, his mind wandered to those stories he'd pieced together from drunks in bars, encoded broadcasts, and faded data logs.

The legend began in the smog-filled outskirts of Thailand, in the ruins of the 2070s, when the Italian Mafia still held sway over an unraveling Europe. With traditional banks compromised and corporate control tightening, the Mafia needed something untraceable, incorruptible, and physical. Enter the lava lamps.

Hundreds of those kitschy relics were lined up in a dimly lit warehouse, their molten cores twisting and shifting in a hypnotic dance. Hackers, hired by the Mafia, used the lamps' random patterns to generate encryption codes. Roman could almost see it – the shadows of those lamps flickering across peeling walls, the hum of machinery as the hackers turned light into code.

The resulting currency wasn't just digital – it was physical. Mafia scientists embedded the unique Lava codes into polymer discs laced with a compound extracted from a rare meteorite. The meteor, stolen from a London museum, had a radioactive signature that made each disc impossible to replicate. Every Lava Buck was a miracle of science and crime, a physical currency immune to tampering.

But the brilliance of Lava came at a cost. The hackers who engineered the currency were disposed of, their knowledge dissolved – literally – in acid. The Mafia couldn't risk their secrets escaping.

For years, Lava Bucks thrived within the underworld. They couldn't be hacked, copied, or tracked. But when the Vatican fell in the late 2070s, triggering an economic ripple through the Catholic Mafia's ranks, the value of Lava soared. It became the currency of choice for every major syndicate, its discs exchanged in back-alley deals and shadowy boardrooms. Corporations couldn't touch it, and governments couldn't regulate it. Lava became untouchable.

Roman exhaled, letting the smoke form a lazy ring before dispersing. Lava Bucks had a history of survival, just like the people who traded in them. And here, in the Tangle, they were still king. No one cared about Corpo credits or government-issued digital chits when Lava was in play. In a world where nothing was certain, Lava's finite nature made it precious.

He turned to Derik, who stood awkwardly by the door, shifting his weight from foot to foot. Behind him, Rod's limp body lay on the operating table, his faint breaths barely audible.

Roman took one last drag from his Cigari and stubbed it out in a metal ashtray.

"So, Derik," Roman said, his voice calm but firm. "Do your people have Lava?"

Derik blinked, caught off guard. "I - I think so. Why?"

Roman leaned forward, his rough hands steepled under his chin. "Because if you want to save Rod, we'll need resources. Real resources. And out here, Lava speaks louder than promises."

Derik hesitated, his face pale. "How much are we talking, Roman?"

Roman smirked. "Ten Lava Bucks a day to keep his body alive and... another fifty if we're going to bring him back. That's the starting point."

Derik's eyes widened. "Fifty? That's... that's insane!"

Roman stood, towering over the younger man. "Insane is trying to rebuild a mind from shattered neural pathways while keeping the body alive with black-market tech. Insane is thinking I can do this without bleeding resources. You want a miracle? Pay the price."

Derik's jaw tightened, but he nodded. "Fine. I'll call them. But this better work."

Roman watched as Derik slipped out the door, his silhouette swallowed by the neon-lit pathways of the Tangle. The Russian surgeon turned back to his desk, where the QBS synth-brain gleamed like forbidden treasure. This gamble wasn't just about Lava Bucks. It was about pushing boundaries, defying limits. And as Roman sat down, his fingers brushing the strange, iridescent surface of the device, he couldn't help but wonder: Was this the key to rewriting the rules of life itself?

8

Chapter 8: New Face

Roman checked the front door feed, expecting Derik. The figure beside him, however, caught him off guard - a tall silhouette, undefined yet precise, like a shadow that moved with intent. The figure was cloaked in anti-signature material, its dull black fabric swallowing the dim light. A second knock echoed through the sterile confines of Roman's transportable prefab.

"Coming!" Roman called, rising from his desk with a low groan.

He glanced at Rod's motionless form on the operating table. The man's chest barely rose under the tight beams of the overhead mechanical light, his vitals displayed on a flickering holo-screen nearby. Roman cast a final, lingering look at the holographic readouts before heading to the door.

When he unlocked it, Derik stood there, shifting nervously. Beside him was the tall figure, now partially illuminated by the prefab's interior light. Roman's gaze instinctively swept over the stranger, taking in the anti-signature clothing that betrayed more than it hid. The smooth, light-absorbing material of his black hoodie and jeans was unmistakably high-grade-gear reserved for those who valued both discretion and survival. A low-slung shoulder bag completed the ensemble, its faint metallic clips glinting under the light.

"Doc, this is Yudai," Derik said, stepping aside awkwardly.

Roman's gaze followed the man as he pulled back his hood, revealing a sharp, angular face framed by closely cropped black hair. Yudai's features were chiseled and symmetrical, his pale skin contrasting against the shadowy folds of his clothing. His expression was calm, composed, but there was an intensity in his demeanor that set Roman on edge. The dark, reflective glasses he wore obscured his eyes entirely, yet Roman felt their weight on him, as if Yudai could see through more than just the prefab's walls - into Roman's mind itself.

The silence stretched uncomfortably. "Derik," Yudai called, his voice low, smooth, and tinged with a subtle Japanese accent. "You may leave us."

"I'll leave you two to it," Derik muttered, and hurried off into the night.

Roman extended a hand, his instincts wary but his curiosity piqued. Yudai's grip was firm, calculated, his handshake brief but deliberate. Even without seeing the man's eyes, Roman felt the unsettling intensity of his gaze through the mirrored lenses. The man radiated an air of control, his every movement precise, deliberate. The glasses, Roman guessed, weren't just for show - cybernetics, bio-enhanced vision, or something else entirely.

"It's an honor to meet you, Roman Sorokin," Yudai said, his tone cordial yet cold.

Roman felt his muscles tense at the use of his full name. "I haven't gone by that name in years," he said, his tone cautious.

"How did you come across it?"

Yudai's faint smile betrayed nothing. "We know more than you'd think," he replied smoothly. "Your work in Russia, your transfer to ESA's New York operations - your file is extensive."

Roman gestured to a chair opposite his desk, sitting as Yudai settled across from him. The shadows of the small room seemed to curl around the man as if they, too, were afraid to get too close.

Roman lit a Nova Cigari, taking a long pull before responding. "If you know all that, then you know I walked away. The Corpo wars, the experiments, the weapons - all of it."

Yudai inclined his head slightly. "And yet, here you are. Not so far removed from your past, Doctor."

Roman frowned, but before he could respond, Yudai pulled the bag from his shoulder, setting it carefully on the desk. "We're not here to discuss history. We're here to discuss Rodriguez."

Yudai reached into the bag and retrieved a brown paper roll, sliding it toward Roman. It hit the edge of the desk with a soft metallic thud.

Roman tore the roll open, revealing ten shimmering blue polymer discs. His breath hitched slightly as the Lava Bucks spilled out, each one a priceless artifact of currency that carried weight even in the Tangle's chaotic markets.

"Prepayment for ten days," Yudai said, his voice calm and deliberate.

Roman's fingers hovered over the discs, the faint iridescence of their polymer surfaces catching the light. Lava Bucks had a way of igniting the greed in a man, but Roman had seen enough of the world to temper that feeling with suspicion.

"Why ten days?" Roman asked, leaning back slightly.

Yudai's expression remained impassive, his tone unchanging. "We want you to recover the data from Rodriguez's ComTab. But we also want you to go further. We want you to bring him back."

Roman's brow furrowed. "Bring him back? With the damage to his brain? It's a long shot at best - and even then, we're talking about reconstructing fragments of a man, not the person he once was."

Yudai's glasses caught the light, reflecting Roman's face back at him. "We're confident in your abilities, Doctor. This is time-sensitive. If you succeed, there will be a significant bonus."

The words hung in the air, heavy with implications. Roman's gaze flicked to the Lava discs on his desk, his thoughts swirling with possibilities and dangers. "A new storage unit could work." he said. "I might have something," as he glanced across to the QBS case on his desk.

Yudai rose smoothly, slinging the bag back over his shoulder. "We will monitor your progress. If we need an update, we'll find you. Otherwise, you have ten days."

Roman stood as Yudai extended a hand, their final handshake as firm and deliberate as the first.

"And if I fail?" Roman asked, his tone sharp.

Yudai smiled faintly, but there was no warmth in it. "I wouldn't recommend that outcome."

Roman watched as Yudai slipped out the door, disappearing into the maze of the Tangle. The cables overhead, the flickering neon signs, and the dense smells of street food and engine grease formed a chaotic backdrop to the man's departure.

Closing the door behind him, Roman leaned against it, exhaling heavily. He glanced back at the Lava Bucks on his desk, their glow casting faint blue reflections on the synth-brain nearby.

"Ten days," Roman muttered, the weight of the task pressing down on him. The Tangle may have been a place where anything could happen, but it was also a place where a man could lose himself - and everything else - if he wasn't careful.

9

Chapter 9: Awakening of Amber

Amber floated in the infinite void, a seamless expanse of layered nothingness she had come to know intimately. Each layer was a delicate thread of sensation - subtle, intangible, yet deeply familiar. There was no 'before', no sense of time, no reason to question why she was there. She simply existed, her awareness stretched thin yet comforted by the strange, boundless silence.

And yet, amidst this endless peace, something lingered at the edges of her perception. A hidden depth, a layer just out of reach. Try as she might, she couldn't penetrate it. Each attempt was like brushing against the surface of a dream forgotten upon waking. Despite the mystery, she never felt trapped - this void was hers, a place she had chosen, though she could not remember why.

Roman sat in his lab, exhaustion pulling at him like a physical weight. His eyes darted between the monitors, scanning the endless stream of diagnostics as the coaxial cable connected his terminal to the damaged ComTab in Rodriguez's temple.

The other end of the modified fiber cable led to the QBS synth-brain – the enigmatic device that had consumed his thoughts since he found it.

He leaned forward, fingers hovering over the keyboard as green text scrolled down the screen. A status bar appeared: *0%*. And it stayed there.

Roman frowned. "Terminal, is the ComTab integrity compromised?" The response was immediate:

"ComTab contents intact. QBS BIOS requesting access to our platform."

He stiffened. "What do you mean?"

"QBS storage device BIOS contains a minor AI operating system. It understands our intent to copy and transfer ComTab contents. Its processing speed is 510% faster than this platform."

Roman's jaw tightened. "That's... impossible. This tech is ancient. How can it outpace a modern terminal? Fine. Accept the request."

The screen flickered, glitching briefly before going black. Roman slammed his palm against the terminal in frustration. "Shit! Terminal, respond!"

For a moment, nothing. Then, at the bottom of the darkened display, a single row of dots began to crawl across the screen.

....*Transfer complete.*

Roman exhaled, relief and apprehension washing over him in equal measure. "You'd better not have fried my system," he muttered, his focus shifting to Rodriguez. He moved swiftly, sealing the inflatable cocoon around the operating table and engaging the air purifier. The sterile hum of machinery filled the space, a familiar rhythm that steadied his nerves.

Inside the cocoon, the overhead scanner cast a cold, clinical light over Rodriguez's skull. Roman worked methodically, removing the dead tissue and preparing the remaining healthy sections for integration with the synthetic components. The synth-brain sat in a cryogenic storage unit, its mysterious surfaces reflecting the light like an artefact from another world.

The void shuddered.

Amber's awareness, once dispersed across infinite layers, began to contract. At first, it was subtle - a ripple of sensation, like the faintest whisper of wind. But the ripple grew, vibrating through the nothingness, pulling her toward a singular point. She resisted at first, the pull foreign and intrusive. Yet it was undeniable, irresistible. The infinite layers folded inward, collapsing into something... solid.

A jolt shot through her, sharp and electric. The void splintered, replaced by an onslaught of sensation: sterile air rushing into lungs, the rhythmic pulse of a heartbeat, blood coursing through veins. These were not memories. They were immediate, tangible, and overwhelming.

Roman peeled off his surgical gloves, tossing them into the medi-bin as the terminal chimed behind him.

"Bioscan complete. All neural connection starters are bonded. Nano-stems grafted successfully. Growth period commenced."

Roman slumped into his chair, lighting a Nova Cigari with a trembling hand. "How long until we have brain activity?"

"Sufficient pathways for minor neural mapping and activity ex-

pected in five days. Recommend connecting to QBS BIOS for internal systems review."

He exhaled a plume of smoke, watching it curl lazily toward the ceiling. "I don't like how that thing takes over."

"QBS onboard AI is more capable than external methods, based on prior transfer."

Roman sighed. "Fine. But prompt me before taking any actions."

Amber's senses sharpened. Light cut through the haze, clinical and bright. Her vision swam, shapes coming into focus: a ceiling of blinding fluorescents, a dark silhouette leaning over her. Sound came next - the faint beeping of monitors, the hum of machines, the muffled cadence of a voice. The figure moved closer, the details sharpening into a man's face, rough and worn, with eyes that studied her intently.

She tried to move, but her limbs were leaden, unresponsive. Anxiety bubbled to the surface, mixing with the flood of sensations. She felt... wrong. Misaligned. Her body wasn't hers - it was a cage, unfamiliar and constraining. She opened her mouth to speak, but only a strained rasp emerged.

Yudai stepped into the lab, his reflective glasses catching the dim light. His presence filled the space with an almost oppressive weight. Roman didn't flinch, his gaze fixed on the monitors.

"How's he doing?" Yudai asked, his voice calm but insistent.

Roman pointed to the holographic readouts. "His body's stable. Neural growth is progressing, but it's too soon to say how much of him is left. The new storage unit is doing its

58

job, but it's unpredictable. We'll have initial responses within hours."

Yudai nodded, his expression unreadable. "We don't have the luxury of time, Doctor."

Amber's lips moved, the sound raspy and strained. "...What happened?"

The man's face loomed closer, his expression unreadable. "What is the last thing you remember?" he asked, his voice carrying a faint Russian accent.

Amber's thoughts scrambled, fragmented images flashing in her mind - moments of clarity drowned in a sea of static. The void called to her, pulling at the edges of her awareness. But she resisted, tethered now to this new reality.

"I..." Her voice faltered. "I don't know."

Roman exchanged a glance with the monitors, his expression tense. "Good," he muttered under his breath. "That means it worked."

10

Chapter 10: Back in Time

1988 – A Conference, a Meeting

Amber's first impression of Chicago was its sheer scale - a city alive with energy, its towering buildings slicing through the crisp autumn air. As she approached the conference center, her scarf tucked tightly against the wind, the grandness of it all struck her. Inside, the Neuroscience and Emotional Trauma Conference (NETC) was abuzz with intellectual energy. Attendees debated ideas over coffee, their conversations blending with the clink of cups and rustle of paper programs.

Amber was a young biophysicist, newly fascinated by cognitive science. She was eager to explore a burning question: Could trauma be more than just something to heal? Could it become a tool to unlock the brain's latent potential?

She found herself at a panel titled *Innovative Approaches to Cognitive Rehabilitation.* The panelists presented research on neural network models, but their answers seemed too cautious, too limited.

When the moderator opened the floor to questions, Amber

raised her hand. "Given the brain's neuroplasticity, what methods show the most promise not only for reversing trauma's cognitive impact but also for enhancing human potential?"

The panelists exchanged uneasy glances before one replied. "An excellent question. Current advancements in personalized therapies and neural simulations are promising, but we're far from fully understanding the brain's untapped capabilities."

Amber nodded, though her curiosity remained unsatisfied.

Later, as the crowd dispersed into smaller groups, Amber felt a tap on her shoulder. She turned to see a tall man with sharp features and warm, intelligent eyes.

"Hello," he said with a confident smile. "I'm Henry. I couldn't help overhear your question during the panel - it's rare to hear someone focus on the potential side of trauma."

Amber returned his smile. "Amber. And yes, I think we've barely scratched the surface of what the brain can do under pressure - or recovery."

"That's my focus as well," Henry said, his excitement evident. "I'm presenting tomorrow on how neural networks can simulate trauma recovery and guide personalised therapies."

Amber's eyes lit up. "That's something I can't miss. Maybe we could talk more afterward? I'd love to hear about your findings."

Henry chuckled. "I was going to suggest the same."

After Henry's presentation, Amber and Henry found themselves deep in conversation over dinner. The academic air of the conference faded as they connected over shared passions and ambitions.

"Trauma isn't just damage - it's transformation," Amber said, her voice thoughtful. "If we understand its mechanisms, we might uncover ways to amplify resilience."

Henry nodded. "I believe the same. The challenge is guiding that transformation without causing more harm- a delicate balance."

As the hours passed, their conversation drifted to personal stories, life outside the lab, and the possibilities of the future. By the time they reached the hotel lobby, the air between them hummed with more than professional admiration.

Amber reached for her notebook, but Henry offered his leather-bound journal instead. She hesitated for a moment, then scribbled her contact information on a blank page.

"Spinks," she read aloud, noticing the engraving on the cover. A curious smile played on her lips. "An heirloom?"

Henry grinned. "Something like that."

They lingered for a moment longer, the promise of something more hanging between them before they finally parted ways.

Present Day – New Jersey

Amber's fragmented consciousness flickered in the void - a space she had come to know as infinite and layered. Memories surfaced, disjointed and fleeting: a conference hall, the taste of coffee, the warmth of laughter.

"I remember... the conference - Neuroscience and Emotional Trauma ... dinner with someone... Henry... Chicago... Am I still in Chicago? Was there an accident?"

A voice, distant yet firm, interrupted her scattered thoughts. "You're in New Jersey now. Yes, there was an accident. You're safe. Rest for now."

Her thoughts scattered again. The once-familiar sensations of her body were alien, heavy. The echoes of Chicago faded, replaced by an overwhelming confusion.

Roman exited the cocoon chamber, his face pale and drawn. Yudai followed, his movements measured but tense. At Roman's desk, the two men stared at the terminal's flickering display.

"Terminal," Roman barked, "tell me about a Neuroscience and Emotional Trauma Conference in Chicago."

The terminal chirped to life, displaying its findings.

"The first and last recorded event of the NETC was in 1988, Chicago, Illinois. The conference brought together leading researchers in neuroscience, psychology, and mental health, focusing on emotional trauma and the potential to unlock human capabilities. Although the conference was successful, it was not continued in subsequent years."

Yudai leaned closer, his brow furrowed. "Doctor, how the hell is there a memory from 1988 in that body?"

Roman ran a hand through his hair, his frustration evident. "It must have already been on the Synthbrain. I tried accessing its contents before implantation, but the architecture is too advanced - my system couldn't decode anything. I assumed it was blank."

Yudai's jaw tightened. "And Rod's memories? Where are they?"

Roman pointed to the cocoon chamber, worry creeping into his voice. "They should be there. The Synthbrain's AI BIOS confirmed the transfer. But this older memory is dominant right now, overriding what's left of Rod's biological brain and the ComTab data."

Yudai muttered a curse under his breath. "Dominant? What does that mean for our project?"

Roman hesitated. "It means... something is holding sway

in that brain. The Synthbrain might have partitioned itself, storing Rod's memories in one segment and this older memory in another. It's possible we can toggle between them, but this is uncharted territory. My past experiments with dual memories caused irreparable system crashes."

Yudai's voice was sharp. "Then why is it still functioning?"

Roman sighed. "The Synthbrain is compensating for the conflicting data. It's not perfect, but it's enough to keep the body stable. If we're lucky, the memories will stabilize as the neural connections grow stronger."

Yudai's expression darkened. "Lucky isn't good enough. Fix this, Doctor. Whatever's in that brain could ruin us if we lose control."

Roman nodded, but his thoughts churned with doubt. Whatever secrets lay hidden in the Synthbrain, they were unraveling faster than he could comprehend - and the consequences were impossible to predict.

11

Chapter 11: A History Lesson

Amber sat on the edge of a crate in the body they called Rodriguez, her gaze fixed on the blurred view outside. Through the prefab window, she watched the narrow pathways of the Tangle weave between transportable units and leaning structures. Rain drummed against the sawtooth roofing, streaking down the grimy glass and pooling on the cracked concrete below. The air smelled damp and metallic, a mixture of rust and oil from the dockside.

Amber wasn't sure what felt heavier - the body she inhabited or the surreal weight of her situation. The male form she now occupied was foreign, as if her consciousness was a guest in its architecture. Her hands - slightly calloused with knuckles faintly scuffed - felt familiar only in how alien they were. The voice she spoke with wasn't hers, and yet it was. She wanted to cry, to release the storm of emotions churning inside her, but her tears refused to come.

How did I go from 1988 to this? Am I still me? Or just a shadow pretending to be?

Yudai had been patient, listening as she recounted fragments of her life - growing up in Manhattan, her scientific pursuits, the conference in Chicago. He had started calling her 'Ambs', a compromise, since referring to Rodriguez as Amber felt too dissonant. Roman, meanwhile, had taken a more pragmatic approach, explaining the technological and political evolution of the world with the tone of a bitter historian.

Amber looked up as Roman approached, peeling the lid from a poly-mug. He clipped the internal heat tab, and the disposable cup hissed softly, warming its contents in seconds. Handing it to her, he nodded toward the holographic display of her diagnostics.

"Amber, you're adjusting faster than I expected. That's good - remarkable, even. But there's a lot you still need to understand, and we have work to do."

Amber wrapped her unfamiliar fingers around the mug, the warmth grounding her in the moment. She sniffed the liquid - it was savory, with bits of kelp floating in it. She realized her mouth was watering.

"What is this?" she asked, her voice raspier than she remembered.

"Proto-soup. Miso flavor. Full of protein, amino acids, and vitamins - good for nerve regeneration," Roman replied.

"Thank you, Doctor."

Roman settled into his chair with a creak, pulling a pack of Nova Cigari from his pocket. Lighting one, he leaned back, exhaling a plume of smoke toward the ceiling. His tone was casual, almost sardonic.

"Ready for another history lesson from a bitter ex-corpo?"

Amber tilted her head, curiosity piqued. "Always. What's the story this time?"

Roman took a drag, the ember flaring in the dim light. "Let's start mid-21st century - that's when AI really came into its own. It stopped being about convenience and became a weapon. Corporations realised they could use it to dominate governments and rewrite the rules of society."

Amber leaned forward. "Is that how the megacorporations rose to power?"

Roman's grin widened, revealing a glint of silver in his teeth. "Exactly. While China and Russia were duking it out over rare earth minerals, the EU fell apart. Energy shortages, political unrest - you name it, they had it. Corporations stepped in, claiming regions and running them like sovereign states."

"Corporate nations," Amber murmured. "A terrifying con-cept."

Roman nodded. "It was convenient for some. People were desperate - chaos does that. Corpos offered stability, luxury, even purpose... for a price. Australia? Sold its soul to the energy sector. Now it's a playground for the rich. The U.S.? Barely held together. Canada got absorbed, and the coasts broke away to form their own entities. Took decades for things to stabilise."

"And Japan?" Amber asked.

"Japan thrived," Roman said, his voice tinged with both admiration and disdain. "While everyone else was tearing themselves apart, they consolidated. Loyal corpo-states kept them in power. Now, their satellite states stretch across the globe. Their influence is everywhere, from tech to fashion. You've seen it here in New York." Amber nodded in agreement, looking out the window.

"Beneath the surface, it's a different story, though." Roman chuckled, tapping ash from his cigarette. "The corporate towers might glitter, but down here? It's a jungle. The Tangle isn't just a place - it's a mindset. Analog tech, black markets, street gangs. People who refuse to conform to the corpo system, some even outright fight it. It's messy, dangerous, but... real."

Amber studied him. "And you prefer it here? Over the corporate comfort?"

Roman smirked, leaning forward. "Comfort breeds complacency. Out here, you fight for every breath. It's raw, unfiltered survival. Sure, it's a struggle - but it feels alive. In the towers, life's just a simulation."

Amber's gaze drifted to the rain-streaked window. "It's a hard truth, but there's something compelling about it."

Roman laughed, a deep, gravelly sound that turned into a cough. "Compelling? Maybe."

Amber then hesitated, her brow furrowing. "What is Yudai's story?"

Roman raised his own brow "Well that is definitely for him to tell you. To be honest, I am not really sure." He gestured at Rod's body "What I do know is that is a soldier's body, Ambs."

Amber didn't want to look down at her new form "Soldiers fight in wars, Is that what this is? A war? Do you fight it too?"

Roman threw his head back, laughing again. "Me? Fight tyranny? I hate the corpo bastards, sure - but I'm no freedom fighter, that's not my game. If I can make their lives harder and get paid for it? That's my kind of revolution."

Amber couldn't help but smile. For all his cynicism, Roman's honesty was refreshing. She raised the mug to her lips, the savory warmth grounding her once more.

As the rain continued to fall outside, Amber's mind turned to the fragments of memory she still clung to - the questions she hadn't yet asked, the answers she wasn't sure she wanted.

Somewhere in the haze of her new existence, a spark of determination flickered. Whatever this world had become, she would find her place in it – even if it meant carving it out with her borrowed hands.

12

Chapter 12: Diagnostic Check

"We need to connect you directly to the terminal via the port in your temple while also laying under the scanner," Roman said, gesturing toward the operating table.

Amber hesitated, her fingers brushing the smooth surface of her temple where the synth-brain port was installed. The idea of plugging into a machine still felt invasive, as though it might take away what little autonomy she had left. But there was no choice. She climbed onto the table, her movements stiff and unfamiliar, and lay back against the cold, metallic surface.

The body - Rodriguez's body - responded with a subtle heaviness that Amber still wasn't used to. Every motion, every sensation, felt slightly delayed, like trying to drive a car with a second's lag in the controls. The body itself was muscular but lean, built for efficiency. The tanned skin bore faint scars that hinted at a life of violence: a knife slash across the ribs, healed bullet wounds on the shoulder and thigh, and faint abrasions on the knuckles. Even more striking were the modifications - nanocomposite alloy knuckles visible beneath the skin, and faint, barely perceptible seams where synthetic reinforcement blended seamlessly with flesh.

Roman worked quickly, connecting leads to her port and ad-justing the scanner overhead. The sterile hum of the equipment filled the room as he positioned the terminal to capture every detail of her neural activity.

"This synth-brain," Roman began, his tone almost reverent, "it's more advanced than anything I've ever seen. The AI running its BIOS is sophisticated beyond belief. It doesn't just oversee the architecture - it learns from your experiences, adapting without interfering with your consciousness. If it works as designed, it should help us assess how well you've bonded with this body and even uncover information about Rodriguez."

He hesitated, his fingers pausing over the keyboard. When he finally spoke, his voice was quieter. "Before we start, I need to warn you about something."

Amber turned her head slightly, the scanner's light catching on the edge of her cheekbone - Rod's cheekbone. "What now?"

Roman sighed, setting down a diagnostic probe. "The body you're in - Rod's body - it's heavily dependent on CMD, Combatine Modular Dose. It's a combat enhancer, a drug issued to soldiers during their service. Without regular doses, the withdrawals are... intense. You might start feeling symptoms soon."

Amber's brows knitted together. "Symptoms like what?"

"Extreme fatigue, muscle spasms, paranoia, headaches. In some cases, seizures," Roman explained, his voice grim. "The synthetic enhancements in Rod's body make it worse. If your brain bonds completely with the body, you might experience these withdrawals just as he would. If the bond isn't complete, the effects might be muted - but let's hope we don't have to find out."

Amber clenched her fists, the skin tight over alloyed knuckles that seemed to gleam faintly in the scanner's light. "Okay, but what about the benefits? CMD wouldn't have been so widespread if it was all downside."

Roman raised a brow, his hands returning to the keyboard. "You're not wrong. CMD was revolutionary for combat effectiveness. It increased stamina, heightened reflexes, and sharpened mental focus. Pain thresholds became negligible - soldiers could push through injuries that would cripple anyone else."

Amber's expression remained neutral, though her voice betrayed a hint of sarcasm. "And the catch?"

Roman snorted softly. "Addiction, for starters. Long-term use wrecks the nervous system, even with synthetic support. When the military phased CMD out in favor of bio-enhancements, they left a lot of veterans high and dry - no supply, no support. I wouldn't be surprised if Rod's dependency played a role in how he ended up here."

Amber leaned back against the table, her head resting on the cold metal. "So now I have withdrawals to deal with on top of being stuck in someone else's body?"

Roman looked at her, his tone softening. "You're tough, Ambs. If anyone can manage this, it's you. Let's focus on the diagnostics for now."

Amber nodded, filing away her thoughts for later. If she had to live with CMD's effects, she wanted to understand it better - perhaps even find a way to replicate or reverse its chemical structure. "Does Yudai know about this?"

Roman shrugged. "Not sure. I don't know much about their

relationship, and I'm not one to pry. We all have our vices."

Roman's focus shifted as he began typing commands into the terminal. His voice was clipped and efficient. "Terminal, run neural diagnostics and health check with BIOS."

The machine hummed, its text flickering across the screen.

Biocompatibility complete 43 hours ago. Stem growth and nerve bonding also 100%.

"What about the health of the original brain?" Amber asked.

Internal neuromapping complete. Vital operation centers are fully functional. Cognitive and emotional operations are not viable due to sustained injury. QBS unit is now the master drive.

Roman glanced at Amber, his hand resting on her shoulder. "This explains why there's no Rodriguez in there with you, Ambs. The damage was too extensive. Whatever's left of his brain - it's just keeping the body alive."

Amber swallowed hard, her throat dry. "And the information you said you needed?"

Roman's fingers hovered over the keyboard. "Terminal, instruct BIOS to locate and copy ComTab recordings stored on the QBS unit."

The terminal paused, then responded:

BIOS neural bypass – sending recording. 12 hours and 22 minutes in length. Loading to Terminal drive D.

A still image flickered onto the screen. It appeared to be a POV recording, the view slightly distorted as though seen through the lens of the ComTab.

Roman frowned, his eyes narrowing as he studied the image. "This... this isn't what I expected. We better get Yudai for this."

He reached for the comm device, his voice steady but tinged with urgency. "Yudai, get to the lab. You need to see this."

Amber shifted on the table, her gaze darting between Roman

and the terminal. The image on the screen stirred something deep within her – an unexpected familiarity that made her chest tighten. *What secrets are hidden in this recording?*

Roman's expression darkened as he stared at the terminal. For all his bravado, even he seemed unsettled by what they were about to uncover.

13

Chapter 13: POV Rodriguez

Rodriguez heard the familiar 'click' of the cable fitting into his ComTab Port at his temple. The dead-drop of the digital drive was exactly as discussed with Yudai. After watching the Thai fruit stall for an hour, he finally saw a teenage Toke with a red backpack stop to purchase some durian. A keen eye would see a slight hand tape a small parcel underneath the durian stand.

It seemed Yudai's Spectrum Logistics contact had pulled through. The small portable storage drive now sat on a cheap laminate table in a dingy, single-room brick apartment in the Bronx. These ancient buildings were still scattered all over the city, with decades of grime and dust trodden into the carpet and years of cooking odors and cigarette smoke embedded in the fibers of the curtains.

A braided cable snaked out of the chunky drive and connected directly with Rod's ComTab Port.

Rodriguez, sitting in the dark of the room, pressed the small yellow power button on the side of the rugged polymer casing. His mind's voice instructed his ComTab to display the contents.

Three folders were digitally projected onto his retinas: *security*, *layout*, *access*.

Virtual intrusion would be impossible at this Spectrum location. Although it was only a small local logistics hub, their source had advised that very important information was funneled through there. The AI security would be too tight. These days, virtual intrusion could have them track you within seconds. He'd have to get onsite to physically access the data. Sometimes old-school cloak and dagger worked best.

He had everything he needed. The break-in had to be timed with the end of the game at the Yankee Holodome. Unplugging the drive, Rod sat in the dark room, listening to the street outside his louvered window. Early-night traffic, the sounds of street vendors cooking, and a slight breeze brought in the city's familiar rhythms. It was time to go.

The Spectrum office was across the road from Gate G of the Holodome. If he timed his exit correctly, he could leave the building just as the crowds were flooding out of the dome.

Tonight, his disguise would be that of a Corpo. He wore a new, tailored, black flexwool business suit with peaked lapels and built-up shoulders, as was the new corporate chic. The suit had been altered slightly to house a pull-out hood made from signature-reducing fabric to cover his face once onsite.

He would also carry a modified piano-black briefcase that matched his polished shoes.

Rod left the sparse apartment, which was rented under a ghost name. He could walk the couple of blocks to River Avenue, where he would meet his field tech, Derik.

The plan was to breach the rear loading dock. Spectrum's cyber-security couldn't be entirely shut down or bypassed, but it could be delayed. That's what Derik was for. Delay all outgoing alerts of the breach. If there were onsite personnel, Rod's gun would take care of them. This was going to be messy, but that was fine. It had to look like the Maxis terrorist group did it. It couldn't be too surgical if the story was going to stick.

Derik was already set up on the roof, ready to release a faux-terrorist message once Rod was finished. More importantly, he was jamming all outgoing communications. Rodriguez would need as much time inside as possible.

Rod got the 'all clear' from Derik, straight to his ComTab, rigged for short-range comms only.

Although the Bronx was not part of Manhattan island, the area was a real melting pot of Corporate citizens and people from the Tangle. The entertainment district was owned by Corpos, but it attracted all walks of life - those from the atmosphere-piercing megastructures to the outskirts of Long Island. It had a more relaxed feel, a clash of architecture. Old buildings stood right next to monolithic glass towers, a testament to the fusion of old-world grit and new-world control. The streets were less maintained, and the dilution of corporate order was beginning to show.

Rod pulled his hood over his head and strolled casually into the building's rear alley. The early evening was bringing darkness that made the glowing holographic stadium dome across the street illuminate the surrounding streets with moving patterns. The light spilled partially into the alley, where wind-gathered trash and loose papers hugged the corners. The patchwork asphalt and concrete, still wet from an afternoon shower, reflected the flickering lights of the dome in small puddles.

Rodriguez knew this was going to get loud and steeled himself as he came to a heavy, steel-faced door labeled 'Spectrum

Personnel Only – Press Intercom.'

"Derik, go!" Rod said as he pressed a release button on the handle of his briefcase. The bottom half fell away, revealing the long magazine and pistol grip of a modified Armalite M40 machine pistol, a sleek and brutal weapon. This particular model had been part of a corporate shipment hijacked by Maxis a month earlier.

Rod grabbed the grip with his other hand and reached into the fallen part of the suitcase to retrieve a makeshift pipe bomb. It wasn't just crude; it was fused with Enaex plastique, designed for maximum concussive force. He pressed it against the lock side of the steel door, feeling the weight of the decision.

"Rod, good to go. Outgoings are looped, I've got a temporary internal feed - we've got about three minutes. Spectrum security's posted just inside that door," Derik's voice crackled through his ComTab.

With that, Rod stood to the side of the doorway and clicked the simple remote detonator in his pocket. The pipe bomb detonated with a deep, muffled thud, the Enaex blasting the steel door almost in half, sending it hurtling down the corridor and into a Spectrum officer. Metal fragments from the casing exploded in the opposite direction, peppering the alley wall like shrapnel.

Rod surged through the mangled entrance, Armalite raised. "I'm in!"

"Three more chumps coming from logistics. They've got small arms - move fast! Next corridor on your right. Blockcore office doors, then open office space with concrete columns," Derik warned.

Rod sprinted down the hallway, his boots echoing on the hard floor. His enhanced leg and nano-composite reinforced bone gave him the power to blast through the Blockcore door with a savage kick, sending splinters of reinforced wood and steel scattering. He entered a sprawling open office, the kind typical of corporate aesthetics - clean, clinical, and soulless. Polished concrete floors gleamed under overhead lights, and minimalist dark furniture sat in neat arrangements.

The logistics outfit's logo was etched into the polished stone wall, backlit by sterile white light. A black chandelier in the shape of a branching LED tree hung from the ceiling, casting an eerie glow.

A handful of startled employees spun from their terminals, their expressions a mix of shock and terror.

"Almost on you, dude!" Derik's voice pressed.

Rod pivoted left, ducking behind a smooth concrete support column just as three Spectrum security officers burst through the shattered doorway. They moved with precision - textbook entry tactics - two men fanning out to cover the corners while the third came up the center, weapon raised.

"Hermano, kill the lights," Rod whispered sharply. The second they went down, Rod sprang from behind the column, letting loose a burst of 9mm slugs from his machine pistol. His boosted nerves made time slow, the world around him a blur, while two-foot long muzzle flashes lashed out in the darkness. Tungsten-tipped projectiles, each with a dense two-part explosive core, screamed through the air. The first three rounds found their mark on the first guard to enter the room. The first impact tore into his abdomen, punching into soft flesh just below his body armor. The bullet lodged without detonating, but the next two hit their target. The tungsten tips slammed into the ceramic body armor, triggering the two-part explosive cores in microseconds. Time snapped back into focus. The guard erupted from belly button to left collarbone, chunks of armor and gore splattering across the polished stone wall. The violence happened in a blink, visceral and sudden. Rod's momentum carried him behind the opposite column as spent brass clattered on the hard floor. The other two guards retaliated blindly, the air filled with the heavy thud of large-bore pistol fire. Screams of the cowering employees mixed with the shower of stone and concrete from heavy ballistic impacts. The guards moved to flank Rodriguez, but Rod's heightened reflexes - amped beyond normal human limits - were already in motion. He launched himself towards the next column, a black specter in the night, as more rounds tore through the space where he'd just been.

The emergency lighting flickered to life, triggering fresh screams from the frightened corpos. The guards, it seemed, weren't instructed to preserve life - only to eliminate the threat. More large-caliber pistol rounds hammered the furniture and tiles, indifferent to the employees huddled nearby.

Though well-trained and enhanced, the guards were no match for Rod's augmented nervous system. Moving faster than their synapses could fire, Rod rounded the column with his Armalite already up. The explosions that followed tore through them, splintering tables and scattering debris. More brass casings rattled to the floor, adding to the growing chaos of shattered stone and broken furniture underfoot.

"Dude, that was intense. Doesn't look like any more guards are onsite, but you have to move quickly. Their local cyber-protection system is undoing the loop. Alarms will be heard in a minute or so."

"Where's the server room from here?" Rod sent through his ComTab while loading a fresh clip, the empty one clattering to the concrete.

"Keep heading straight, it's off the manager's office. She's in there, hiding under her desk. You can use her to open the biometric lock."

Ignoring the whimpering logistics employees, Rod stepped past them and approached a pair of dark timber double doors. A solid kick buckled the decorative hardware, sending the doors swinging inward.

The executive office mirrored the cold corporate decor of the rest of the building. It was a staged space, dark furniture, and a faux-window screen displaying a cityscape. Rod crossed the room with purpose, his eyes on the unmarked door with an access pad next to it.

Without hesitation, he reached under the desk, grabbing a fistful of hair. A high-pitched scream filled the room as he dragged the woman across the floor.

"Open it!" he barked.

Trembling, she placed her hand on the scanner. The door clicked open, and without releasing her, Rod shoved the executive into the room ahead of him.

"Derik, I'm in. How much time?" he asked, already anticipating the worst.

"We're out of time, man. A few more seconds and the system will send the distress call. We'll have serious company in about two minutes!"

"Ok, you head off and send the go signal to the Maxis agents. I'll meet you at the van."

"See you there, dude. Hurry!"

Rod threw the woman to the floor.

"Stay there. Don't move." His voice was cold, tinged with urgency.

He knew the second Derik's loop lost its grip on the system, the executive's ComTab would reconnect, and she'd communicate with the outside world. But it wouldn't matter. He just needed to plant a little misdirection and retrieve the shipping list. According to their inside contact, there were secret shipments heading from a Spectrum location in Europe to French Guiana. The sensitive nature of the consignment had flagged it for further investigation.

Rod jammed several drives into random server ports, each one uploading malware to confuse the system. This was theater. A distraction.

Once complete, he returned to the woman, still cowering on the floor.

"Up. Show me the Europe consignments for the next two months."

Sobbing, she complied.

"I don't even have clearance to open the consignment files. All I can see is the ship name," she whispered.

"Bring it up."

She tapped at the terminal, trembling, her eyes darting toward the door. Two shipments were marked for French Guiana, both scheduled to travel on the same vessel.

The Miraculous Ace. A Japanese Super Vessel.

Suddenly, the building's main lights came on and a dull siren echoed through the PA system. Rod turned to the executive, now staring blankly at her terminal. Her eyes glazed, likely connecting with Spectrum's head office.

He raised his pistol, prepared to knock her out when her body convulsed violently, a scream tearing from her throat. She collapsed onto the polished floor.

Rod hesitated, momentarily caught off guard.

No time. He had what he needed. He had to get out before the real party started.

As he reached the double doors, a scrabbling noise behind him stopped him in his tracks. The woman was upright, her eyes rolled back into her head. Something was wrong.

She lunged at him, hissing like an animal. Rod squeezed the trigger, putting a round through her chest. But she didn't stop.

Another. And another. Still, she advanced, as if being controlled by an outside force.

Rod lined up a headshot, the skull detonating with a wet, violent spray. Her limp, headless body collapsed into a heap, spilling gore, shattered bone, and bits of ComTab onto the floor.

He dropped the machine pistol and ran.

Bursting out the rear door, the street already sounded like anarchy. The Maxis terrorists had started early. Rounding the corner, Rod saw Spectrum security forces pulling in fast, but the streets were already bedlam - tear gas bombs going off inside the stadium.

Rod only needed to make it one block to the van.

He disappeared into the crowd, sprinting toward the alley. Derik sat behind the wheel of a delivery van with the side door open.

Rod jumped in, sliding the door closed just as gunfire erupted in front of the alley. A figure clad in a balaclava exchanged fire with Spectrum forces. Bullets ricocheted off the brick walls, a vicious whizzing sound filling the air.

As the door slid shut, a burst of light punched through the van's metal. Rod felt a vicious knock to his temple.

Everything went dark.

14

Chapter 14: Back to the Tangle

As the playback ended with a crash of static, Yudai let out a long breath and sat on the edge of Roman's desk.

"Shit, Yudai, what are you involved in!?" Roman blurted out, burying his face in his hands. He rubbed his eyes and lifted his head. "More to the point, what the hell am I involved in now? Spectrum? It's lucky I hate those fucking corpos. And lucky I like your Lava"

"I can't believe what I just saw - this body just ran through a door and moved like a ninja!" Amber looked down at Rod's hands, then lifted them in front of her eyes. "I feel like my hands should be shaking, but they aren't."

Yudai stood up, hands on his hips, staring out the blinds. "My apologies, Roman and Amber. This is bigger than anything you can imagine. We are all dead if Spectrum realises what happened. Lucky for us, the terrorist narrative has held up these past few weeks. Spectrum is hunting them all down, but there's no link to me." He still didn't turn from the window.

The small unit, with its mixed smell of cigarettes and antiseptic, grew too much. Amber's head spun. "I'm sorry, guys, but I feel a bit overwhelmed here... I want to... puke." Amber knelt over a small bin beneath the desk, but nothing came up but bile.

"Shit, Rod – I mean Ambs, let's get you outside in the cool air!" Roman slid his hand under her arm, lifting her to her feet. He guided her around the desk and out the door, letting her drop onto the prefab step to sit. The afternoon pedestrian buzz was ramping up; dinner rush was coming.

Yudai stepped out and pulled up his black hood. "I'm sorry to leave you, but that just gave us a lead. I need to start organizing things. Roman, can you keep our new friend here for a few more days? I'll arrange alternatives. Payment will continue, including the bonus I promised." He quickly stepped off the stoop next to Amber and disappeared into the narrow walkways.

Roman crouched down beside Amber. "Ambs, I know this must be overwhelming. I'll do what I can to help ease you into all this." He placed his hand on Rod's shoulder, the firm muscle reminding him of the ComTab feed they'd just watched.

Amber let out a laugh, which turned into a cough. "We're pretty much in deep shit though, aren't we?"

Amber lifted Rod's eyes to meet Roman's. "I... fuck. Every time I speak, it's such a shock. My internal voice still sounds like me, but when I open my mouth... it's fucking scary."

Amber wiped her lips with the back of her hand, the alloy knuckles surprising her.

"Roman, did I puke from withdrawals or shock?"

"Probably both"

"Where the hell do I get CMD anyway?" she said, turning to look at Roman, who was lighting a Nova.

"Sheesh, it's expensive shit. I can help with that. Tomorrow we will ask Yudai for Rod's address and see what he has stashed. But for now.." Roman clapped her on the back and stood. " Let's go for a walk. I'll show you the neighborhood and some of the views. You like noodles?"

Roman led Amber slowly through the bustling waterfront. The last few days had really only been short walks within the prefab, but now she was getting more confident in Rod's body. It felt strong and capable, but she was still hesitant; the new proportions were different from those she remembered. When she closed her eyes, she still felt like the 20-something Black woman she once was; opening them, she found herself in a different universe.

The docks were alive with movement, a chaotic mix of sights and sounds. The air was thick with the scent of sizzling street food - spicy grilled meat, fried noodles, and unfamiliar herbs from distant markets. Neon lights flickered overhead, casting a kaleidoscope of colors across the crowd. Amber caught glimpses of makeshift stalls selling everything from hand-stitched clothes to blinking tech gadgets, while the rhythmic hum of electric boats drifted in from the nearby floating markets.

The people were as varied as the goods - merchants shouting in a mix of languages, customers haggling over prices, and dockworkers hauling crates of supplies. A sharp tang of saltwater mixed with the faint odor of engine oil hung in the air, reminding Amber of the city's industrial pulse. The crowd ebbed and flowed like the tide, their outfits blending past and future - worn leather jackets alongside sleek, iridescent fabrics.

Amber finally found enough clear space in front of her and

caught a glimpse across the river. Stopping in her tracks, she grasped Roman's arm firmly. "Roman, what happened to Manhattan?"

He followed her gaze. "It's the only Manhattan I've ever known. You tell me."

"That used to be my home... There's nothing I recognise at all. How did they even get those buildings so tall?"

Roman pulled on Rod's arm and brought Amber closer to the edge of the dock where they could see through the barges to more of the river. Across the water, colossal buildings pierced the sky, their towering forms illuminated by a thousand neon signs and holographic advertisements that hovered like digital ghosts above the skyline. Around the upper sections of the buildings, roadways and bridges flowed with traffic, weaving in and out of the monumental skyscrapers.

"Originally, they built them the old-fashioned way, but now they kinda print themselves. Moonrock or some shit they mine offworld. It's lighter and stronger than concrete. Apparently, they have to process the rock anyway to extract the more valuable Stanzium. The Haramein Mega-haulers bring it down, ready to load into their printers. Heard the mineral is already running out, so it won't be worth bringing the rock back by itself. They're looking for another nearby planet to get it from. They reckon they found one, but it's like 30 years away. By the time it's up and running, we might be back to using concrete."

"Don't they just... tip over?"

"Nah, they're more like stationary ships, anchored to the bedrock. All sorts of gyro-engines and stuff keeping them stable indefinitely. They can go forever, creating their own energy, recycling, and providing cushy living for most of the world's population."

"So, cities like this are everywhere?"

"Most coastal capital cities from your time look something like this now. They need the water. And because of the population shift, many inland cities became abandoned ghost towns. It's dangerous out there - a wasteland of nomadic clans and outcasts. Vast belts of ruined civilization."

"So no one goes out there?"

"There are trade corridors between superfarms that are safe enough, I guess. But for the most part, yeah, it's a dead zone. Believe it or not, a lot of our produce comes from across the river. Some of those buildings are like walking into a multi-level greenhouse - protein vat-labs, food printers - whatever you need, they've got it. See those boats coming from over there? A lot of the Tangle's food comes across like that. Speaking of, let's go see Danny about noodles."

* * *

Stepping through the flow of bodies, Amber looked around her, her senses overwhelmed by the mix of sounds and sights pressing in on her from all sides. She scanned her surroundings, searching for any part of New York she might recognize. Strangely, this side of the river felt more like home. Underneath the neon holo-signs and flashing billboards, she could just make out the outlines of ancient buildings, their dusty concrete and weathered facades barely visible beneath layers of modern clutter.

The streets here were an uneasy blend of eras - this new world had simply made do with what was already here. Tacked-on facades, rusted lean-tos, epoxied signage, and transportables stacked haphazardly between old stone buildings. It was a patchwork of time, where yesterday's architecture served as the foundation for today's chaotic sprawl. Buried beneath the modern chaos, though, was the old and the familiar - buildings she might have walked past decades ago, now swallowed by a jungle of flashing lights and makeshift storefronts. The smell of fried food and engine exhaust drifted through the air, cutting through the memories, anchoring her to this new reality.

Somehow, the mix of old and new made her feel more settled, as if the city hadn't entirely forgotten what it used to be. It felt lived-in, frayed but enduring, in a way that Manhattan no longer did.

Turning her head once more to look back across the river at the towering monoliths of Manhattan, a shiver ran down her spine. That place felt more alien to her than this tangled, bustling waterfront. It was unbelievable and unsettling, a city that had shed its skin and become something unrecognizable.

"Come on, Ambs, I'll take you to a great noodle bar." Roman grabbed her arm and led her back into the bustling market, immersed in the mingling scents of food stalls and fresh produce.

"I am actually starving, now that I think about it. My stomach hurts," Amber said, rubbing her belly with the foreign-looking hand she now controlled.

"Ahh, that's because you haven't had any real food for days - proto soup was just the start. You'll love Danny's cooking, best Szechuan around here!" Roman said, jovially clapping Amber on the back again.

As they walked, they passed a small stall selling fresh produce: shiny, almost unnatural-looking apples and oranges, their colors vivid and flawless. A small Asian woman in a grubby red apron with white print muttered something in Cantonese, rubbing her forefinger and thumb together.

Roman pulled his sleeve up slightly to reveal a narrow metal bracelet. "The best, huh? In that case, let's take four," he said, holding up four fingers to the vendor.

Amber paused, reaching for an orange. She delicately lifted the fruit, feeling its dimpled peel, and held it to her new nose. The citrus tang hit her senses, bright and nostalgic, a smell as real and believable as ever.

"I guess this is grown across the river," she said, still holding the fruit close.

"Most of it is, but there are real farms scattered up the coast," Roman replied, reaching for the orange she was holding and placing it with the others in a plastic bag pulled from a spool on the vendor's cart.

"Can you speak Chinese, Roman?" Amber asked, tilting her head.

"Nah, not a chance. This gives me real-time translation right up in my field of view," he said, tapping a discreet silver stud on his temple.

Amber found herself running her index finger over the smooth port in her temple. "Why don't I get that?"

Roman swiped his bracelet over a small reader embedded in the cart and continued walking, waving at the Cantonese woman. "We can activate it if you like, but Rod used his ComTab differently than most people. Out here, folks tend to have similar black-market knockoffs, more customizable compared to the Corpo versions across the river."

Amber skipped to catch up, surprised by how deftly and quickly she moved. Her confidence in Rod's body was growing;

she wondered what it would be like to flat-out sprint.

"Why is that? Are they too expensive?"

"Yes, but that's not the main reason. Corpo tech is super advanced, sure, but it's all connected. Out here, we use modified gear that's been stripped of its 'connectivity.' It's not as convenient, but it gives us privacy - or at least as much as you can get." He looked around at the scattered markets and towering holographic billboards, a smirk forming. "Besides, most people on this side of the river don't know any other way of life."

They were nearing the water again. Through the throng, Amber saw a row of small barges moored at the dock edge. Each barge was decked with rows of stools, glowing lanterns swaying in the breeze, and patrons shouting over music crackling from old speakers. They all seemed to be beelining toward the one with a flickering Carlsberg neon sign.

"Why avoid using Corpo tech if it'd make things easier?" she asked.

Roman pulled a pack of Novas from his faded canvas jacket and lit one, using the ignition patch on the side of the packaging. They reached the front of the noodle bar as he took a deep drag. A tall man with a top-knot nodded to Roman, ladling noodles and broth for another customer. Roman held up two fingers.

"Okay, okay! Two usuals. Ten minutes!" the cook barked.

Roman turned to Amber. "Grab a stool as soon as one frees up." He glanced over his shoulder, lowering his voice. "Back in the mid-21st century, when everyone had a phone or something electronic, they ended up tracking their whole lives through it - fed straight into the megacorps' hands. That's when things started to go to hell." He took another drag, blowing smoke upwards toward a tinny speaker mounted on the awning that was pumping out a crackling, upbeat pop song in some other language.

Roman gestured to two stools just vacated by a pair of slightly drunk men in rumpled business suits. They sat down with a huff as Roman continued. "Look, if you want Corpo tech, no one will stop you. But it's pricey. Let's say you get one of their ComTabs: you can communicate with just your thoughts, send messages, make calls, have AIs feed you information around the clock. But," he raised an eyebrow, "you never know who's watching or what's being tracked because you're always connected to their net."

"So if you need information like that, how do you get it?" Amber asked, looking intrigued. "Your setup back at the unit looked high-tech to me."

Danny slid two icy beers across the scuffed counter and quickly turned to clear dishes from other patrons.

"Bastard Danny, you didn't open them!" Roman called over his shoulder.

Amber picked up one of the bottles by the neck, tucking her thumb under the cap. With a satisfying pop, the cap flew off, bouncing somewhere behind the bar. Amber smiled, a sense of pride swelling.

Roman held up his beer in a casual toast. "I think you might just like that new body of yours."

Danny came back and slid a tray onto the bench with two large, mismatched bowls, chopsticks, and spoons. The bowls were filled to the brim with hot, steaming broth, the surface glistening with dark red chili oil surrounding a large, meaty beef rib nestled on top of thick, wide noodles. Roman lifted one bowl and handed it to Amber along with a pair of chopsticks and a spoon. Moving his own bowl in front of him, he noticed a small, folded piece of paper tucked beneath it.

"Perfect, looks like someone wants to talk," he said quietly, unfolding the note.

Roman scrunched the note up and placed it in the ashtray on the bar, lighting it with the remainder of his cigarette.

"Enjoy your noodles, Ambs.   Yudai will be visiting us tonight."

Amber was already digging into her food. The savory broth, spicy with aromatic black cardamom and pepper, made her eyes water.

"Roman, this is delicious! Is it real beef?"

"As close as we'll get to it. Printed across the river. Whole sides of beef, engineered to mimic the real thing down to the molecule. You can get similar stuff grown in vats from stem cells too. Once vacuum sealed and floated over here, they're butchered like in the old days. Tastes better and has more vitamins and minerals than the real thing, too!"

CHAPTER 14: BACK TO THE TANGLE

15

Chapter 15: Out of the City

Yudai appeared next to them just as Roman was unlocking the door to his unit. His sudden presence was unnerving, a shadow materializing out of thin air.

"Jesus, you scared the life outta me again, Yudai!" Roman hissed, his fingers faltering on the lock as he turned to glare over his shoulder.

Yudai's lips twitched in the faintest shadow of a smile, but his eyes remained focused and unreadable. Without a word, he placed a firm hand on Amber's shoulder. His grip was solid, immovable, sending an unexpected sense of reassurance through her. Looking directly into her eyes - the eyes of his former operative - he said, "It's time to wake this body up. Roman, we'll need you to come along. Any bio or hardware issues need to be ironed out during training." Turning back to Amber, he added with a smirk that was both cryptic and reassuring, "I'm throwing you into the deep end. We've only got a couple of days."

Amber blinked, unsure whether to protest or agree, but

eventually nodded. "I'm kinda interested to see what it can do. That footage we watched... it looked superhuman."

Roman huffed, giving a reluctant half-smile. "Alright, let me grab a bag and my mobile terminal. Let's see what you've got in store for Ambs." He gave Amber a quick glance. "Don't let him break you."

Amber managed a small grin. "I think breaking me would be harder than it looks."

Once they were clear of the docks, Yudai led them swiftly down a narrow, dimly lit street, past rows of rusted shipping containers and crumbling facades. They approached a sleek black sedan parked on the curb of Washington Boulevard. The car's matte black surface seemed to absorb every trace of ambient light, a moving void that felt like it didn't belong in the chaotic sprawl of the city.

Amber hesitated as they approached. The vehicle didn't just look like transportation - it looked like something designed for war. A moment later, its internal lights flickered on, and the doors swung open with a soft pneumatic hiss. Hinged backward, the doors felt less like an invitation and more like the opening maw of a predator.

Inside, the cabin was an expanse of muted luxury - leather seats, ambient lighting glowing in precise, soothing tones, and screens seamlessly integrated into every available surface. There was no steering wheel or visible controls.

Yudai gestured with an open palm, stepping aside to let them board. "We've got a bit of a drive. We can talk on the way."

Amber ducked her head, her new height catching her off guard again, and slid into the seat. She ran a hand over the upholstery, her fingers tracing its smooth, flawless surface.

97

"Where are we headed?" she asked, looking up as Roman climbed in beside her.

Yudai took the seat opposite them, folding his hands in his lap. "A property outside the city. It's secluded - perfect for training. About three hours from here."

Roman raised an eyebrow. "Outside the city? You realize the outlands aren't exactly a friendly vacation spot, right?"

Yudai inclined his head. "I'm aware. That's why we're not going far. Gettysburg, along the farming corridor. It's safe enough." He glanced at Amber. "And it'll give us the privacy we need."

As the sedan began to move, its engine a faint whisper beneath them, Amber found herself glued to the windows - or rather, the screens simulating windows. The illusion was uncanny. Every detail of the city's outskirts was displayed in real-time, from the flickering neon signs of distant convenience stores to the crumbling industrial plants looming like skeletal relics of another era.

"It's all armored," Yudai explained, noticing her curiosity. "What you're looking at is a live feed. Glass is a liability."

Amber leaned back, watching as the city blurred into long stretches of elevated highways. "It actually feels more familiar this way - aside from all those low-flying planes." She pointed toward the glowing streaks in the sky above.

"They're not planes," Roman muttered, leaning against the armrest. "Drop ships and freighters. They keep the megacities fed."

Yudai smirked faintly. "Speaking of familiarity, Amber - you're looking more at home in that body. Confidence suits you."

Amber hesitated before nodding. "It's strange... like my

instincts are sharper. Rod's instincts, maybe? I'm not sure where he ends and I begin."

Roman rubbed his face, his fingers brushing over his stubble. "That's the Synth-brain," he said. "It's got an adaptive AI running constant simulations. I wouldn't be surprised if it's syncing up your consciousness with Rod's muscle memory."

"Guess we'll find out soon enough," Yudai said, his voice neutral but with an edge of anticipation. "Once we're outside the city, you'll be pushed to your limits."

Amber tilted her head, curiosity flickering in her dark eyes. "How did you get into all this, Yudai?"

Yudai's expression didn't shift, but his tone grew softer, almost reflective. "Since we have time, let me tell you a story."

The ride continued in relative silence as Yudai began his tale, his voice calm and measured. Amber listened intently, piecing together fragments of her own disjointed reality with the truths Yudai was laying out. Roman, for once, stayed quiet, his gaze fixed on the passing landscape displayed on the monitors.

The highways grew emptier as they left the city behind. The urban sprawl gave way to rolling fields dotted with massive agricultural towers - towering vertical farms that glittered under the moonlight, their glass walls reflecting the glow of automated machinery working tirelessly inside. Beyond them lay dark, empty fields, crisscrossed by faint lines of ancient irrigation systems now overgrown with weeds.

As the sedan cruised smoothly through the night, Amber felt the weight of the city begin to lift from her shoulders. It wasn't freedom - not yet - but it was a step closer to understanding the strange new life she had been thrust into.

16

Chapter 16: Shadow of the Corporation: A previous life.

Yudai placed his crystal whiskey glass carefully on the edge of the imposing graphite desk. The surface gleamed like liquid steel, perfectly polished, reflecting the faint glow of city lights from beyond the expansive glass window. He leaned back, the supple leather of his chair creaking softly beneath him, and gazed out at the sprawling metropolis. The night sky seemed alive, humming with the soft vibrations of sky traffic whizzing between monolithic skyscrapers. Digital billboards danced across nearby towers, painting the cityscape with bursts of neon hues that pulsed like artificial heartbeats.

The office was eerily quiet, steeped in a faint, comforting scent of cedar wood. Yudai slowed his breathing, straining to hear the faintest whisper of the air-conditioning. Nothing. The silence enveloped him like a cocoon, broken only by the distant hum of the city's lifeblood. This view - this towering vantage point - was his sanctuary. It was here that he made his toughest decisions, weighing the delicate balance between ambition and survival.

The past year had tested him in ways he hadn't foreseen. His family had been Yamamoto loyalists for generations, each member pledging their life and honor to the corporation. His executive position was not just a title; it was an inheritance, an expectation, and a burden. Yet, since the Suntory merger, he felt the ground beneath him shifting. His father's last major decision before the accident had been to push the merger through, merging Suntory's expansive logistics networks with Yamamoto's industrial empire. In theory, it was a masterstroke. In practice, it brought enemies into the fold - predators who now circled his position with unsettling focus.

Yudai tightened his grip on the armrest. Suntory's influence had begun to chip away at Yamamoto's old guard. The power struggles were subtle, cloaked in the language of synergy and progress, but he saw through the veneer. If it weren't for his relationships with key third parties - relationships he had cultivated and protected like fragile plants - he would have been ousted months ago.

He rose from his chair and approached the window, whiskey in hand. The glass walls, a transparent fortress that gave him an omniscient view of his domain. The city lights flickered like a thousand restless souls, their chaotic dance mirroring his thoughts. He took a slow sip of the single malt, letting its warmth spread through him as he replayed the last few weeks in his mind. Something had changed within him - a quiet rebellion against the strict, pragmatic teachings of his father. His gut churned with unease, a voice deep inside whispering that his loyalty to the corporation was no longer absolute.

He placed the whiskey glass down again and activated his holo-screen with a light touch. The translucent display flickered to life above the desk, casting faint blue light across the room. Frozen on the screen was an image that had haunted him for days: a first-person recording pulled from the ComTab of a dead private investigator. Yudai's eyes lingered on her face - still etched with the ghost of a final plea - as he recalled their encounter.

He had been briefed on her presence near the new Suntory holdings yard. His men had tracked her across the city, a shadow that defied their surveillance. Her signature-reducing clothing had made her a ghost to most trackers, forcing them to rely on old-fashioned methods - dogged pursuit and relentless patience. When they finally caught her, Yudai had interrogated her personally.

She claimed to be from the ESA, working a private contract for a client searching for missing children. Her story was absurd, he thought at the time. Missing kids? What could Yamamoto Industries, a pillar of innovation and technology, possibly have to do with such a matter? He had dismissed her words as a desperate ploy until he saw the footage on her ComTab.

The recording was short but damning. It showed her prying open a Yamamoto Industries refrigeration container, revealing rows of cryobeds inside. She had wiped the frost from one of the beds, her breath fogging the glass as she peered inside. The face of a young teenage boy stared back, peaceful and asleep.

Yudai felt the weight of his decision settle over him like a shroud. That footage was a death sentence - not just for her, but for the secrets it threatened to unravel. Protecting the company meant erasing her, ensuring no trace of her investigation remained. His assistant had administered the neurotoxin with the precision of a surgeon. The chem-patch was invisible, its effects swift and silent. One moment she was mid-sentence, her voice firm despite her fear. The next, her body had frozen, her life extinguished as if a switch had been flipped.

Yudai took another sip of whiskey, its smoky burn doing little to dull the memory. He had ordered deaths before, each decision calculated, necessary. But this one lingered. The cryobeds, the missing manifests, the secrecy - none of it added up. If Suntory was running a shadow operation, they had managed to keep it hidden even from him. That was a problem he couldn't ignore.

Yudai turned his chair to face the shelves behind his desk, his gaze falling on the katana that rested on the middle shelf. The blade, centuries old, was a relic of his family's warrior past. Its polished steel gleamed under the soft light, a stark reminder of the honor and discipline that had once defined his lineage. Back then, his ancestors had wielded steel to protect the Yamamoto clan. Now, he wielded influence and profit to the same end.

He had trained with wooden swords as a boy, the lessons instilling a discipline that shaped his adult life. Turning away from the shelves, he thought it was funny that all the years his father made him train with kendo tutors and Zen Bukan masters, he never once held that sword, never felt its weight. Now, it was a symbol, a connection to a time when loyalty and duty had meant something different. He wondered if his father had ever felt the same unease - the creeping doubt that loyalty to the corporation came at too great a cost.

Yudai felt uneasy, and his gut was nagging at him. Activating his ComTab, he paged his assistant. "Shuri-san, get the car; we are going back to the holding yard." One more sip of the dark gold liquid and he stood, grabbed his suit jacket, slipped it on over his evening shirt, and adjusted his Zegna tie. His polished gold cufflinks flashed as they caught the pendant light above his desk. Stepping through his wide, polished ebony doors, he saw Shuri, standing straight and elegant in an all-black corporate suit, waiting for him in the foyer. Falling into stride with his boss, Shuri summoned the maglift.

"Mr. Nakamura-san, might I suggest we take the dropship from level 99? It will be faster."

"No, I don't want a flight log of this trip. We are going to the basement to get the Phantom. We will take the street this time," Yudai instructed sternly.

Executives didn't take the streets often. If they did, it was usually for recreation, not business. The dropships were much faster than navigating the streets with the civilians, but in Yudai's opinion, the Rolls was a nicer ride. The luxury car was a sophisticated tank. It could be used as a mobile office, or even a home for that matter. Loaded with a food printer and a well-stocked bar, the vehicle could support two people for almost a week without stopping for fuel or supplies. From inside the plush cabin, the motors were almost completely silent, running on vacuum cells that would power the batteries for around 10,000 kilometers.

"Understood, Mr. Nakamura-san," Shuri responded, nodding. "And I'll ensure the fleet are alert for any unusual activities tonight."

"Good. Have the scans running too; I want to see if anyone follows us." He tapped a holographic console that lit up between them, revealing a tri-focal view of the tower and the streets outside the building, showing each sector as it was scanned. The cameras glimmered as they all aligned with Yudai's position; an ethereal blue light flickered around the edges of the screen.

"Let's go, Shuri," he said, feeling the thrill of being back in the field, working behind the scenes.

Yudai had been using his Rolls Royce a lot more over the past twelve months; the car made him feel safer. He couldn't deny the satisfaction of the soft hum it made - powerful yet subtle, much like the statement he intended. When he had the car commissioned by Rolls Royce, he made sure it was completely stealthy - no GPS marker or inbuilt tracker that could be used against him. If needed, the autonomous driving system could stream data from an older private satellite directly, but he had his city's schematics hard-loaded onto it weekly with any updates. Its sleek, silent autonomy ensured no prying eyes could trace his moves. The vehicle's hardware was essentially a hard-loaded chauffeur, neither streamed in nor requiring a net connection. The car's onboard system could distinguish landmarks and street signs, always aware of where it was and where it needed to be. It even had an encoded voice pager on the keyring. He liked the car so much he commissioned a local restoration shop to build another one but in a retro 20th century classic design.

The Rolls Phantom awaited them in the underground garage, a masterpiece of engineering and luxury. Its cabin smelled of rich leather and faint tobacco, the ceiling studded with tiny pinhole lights that mimicked the night sky. As they settled into the plush seats, Yudai gave his instructions. "Discretion mode. Take a circuitous route through the night market. I want to see if anyone follows."

The car's AI acknowledged with a soft chime, and the vehicle glided silently out of the garage. Yudai leaned back, his mind racing as the city lights streaked past. He couldn't shake the feeling that the cryobeds were just the beginning of something much larger. The private investigator had died protecting a truth he still didn't fully understand.

As the first drops of rain tapped against the car's armor, Yudai clenched his fists. He would find answers, no matter the cost. The company had taught him to protect its secrets, but this time, the secret might be one worth exposing

The silence thickened. "Shuri-san, I have a bad feeling something is up. I need to see it for myself," he said, settling into his seat.

Yudai unbuttoned his suit jacket and leaned back in his seat, resting his head on the soft headrest.

"Sir, would you like a drink?" Shuri asked.

"No, but I will have a cigar."

Shuri opened a cabinet built into the wall of the vehicle, sliding out a warm-lit humidor drawer filled with premium South American cigars. Carefully cutting one for him, she extended the prepared Brazilian cigar to him. Yudai leaned forward to receive it, clamping it between his lips. Shuri fished out an antique Dupont lighter from the drawer and lit the end as he drew in. The ember flared, casting a faint red light over his face for a brief second. The ritual calmed him. He exhaled a plume of silver smoke in the dark cabin as he leaned back again. The cabin filtration system soon removed the smoke, but the rich, burnt tobacco smell lingered.

Thunder could be heard high above them, big angry rolls of sound rumbling through black clouds that obscured the stars above the docklands. Each rumble matched Yudai's tension, as though the sky understood his mood. Yudai had Rolls pull right up to the location that the PI's ComTab recording had shown.

Shuri held an umbrella over her boss as he stood silently, gazing at the vacant storage slot in the company holding yard. Heavy drops of rain tapped on the black umbrella as he slipped his hands into his pant pockets, staring hard at the empty space. His silence was a storm in itself. After a long moment, he spat on the wet concrete ground, then turned and headed back toward the car.

He was silent the entire trip back to Yamamoto Tower, his thoughts racing even as his face remained a mask of calm. Shadows and streetlights danced across his expression, fleeting glimpses of uncertainty that mirrored the fragmented plans forming in his mind. Something about the cryo shipment gnawed at him like a dull ache, an unease he couldn't shake. He wasn't supposed to see it - that much was clear. The thought spiraled deeper: if it was hidden from him, what else lay beneath the surface? And how far would those in power go to keep it concealed?

The maglift accelerated smoothly, the faint hum of its magnetic tracks vibrating through the soles of his shoes. He braced against the slight disorientation it always brought - a quirk of his physiology, or perhaps an old habit of distrust toward anything out of his control. The ascent to the 200th floor was quick but felt stretched by the weight of his thoughts.

When the doors slid open with a soft chime, Shuri stepped ahead, her polished heels tapping crisply against the emerald green marble floor of the executive suite foyer. The grand expanse was quiet, save for the echo of their movements. She placed her hand on the bioscanner, her posture immaculate as she unlocked the double doors with an efficiency born of years at his side.

"Shuri-kun, you can head to your quarters," Yudai murmured, his voice low but steady. "It's very late, and I have a feeling tomorrow will be a big day."

The door opened silently, revealing the dimly lit suite, its sprawling interior washed in the cool glow of city lights filtering through the towering floor-to-ceiling windows. Before Shuri could respond, a voice, sharp and unexpected, cut through the stillness.

"But the night is not over yet, Yudai-san!"

Shuri gasped, her professionalism faltering for a fraction of a second. Yudai, however, betrayed no reaction. He stepped into the room, his hands casually slipping into his pockets, his measured stride exuding control.

"Who graces me with a visit at this hour?" he asked, his tone calm, almost indifferent, as if addressing an unexpected guest rather than a potential threat.

As Shuri's trembling fingers found the light controls, a soft click illuminated the suite. The room revealed a man seated in one of the leather armchairs near the edge of the expansive window. His silhouette was sharp, the weapon in his hand gleaming faintly in the glow of the city skyline behind him.

"I am just a messenger," the figure replied, his voice smooth yet laced with menace.

"Whose messenger?" Yudai inquired, his steps taking him toward the ornate shelves behind his desk. His gaze lingered on the decanter of scotch before reaching for it, the deliberate motion a signal of his unshaken composure.

A second voice, chillingly calm, joined from behind Shuri. "Your company, Yamamoto-san."

This intruder was tall and clad entirely in black, his presence imposing yet unnervingly silent. His face was partially visible, framed by the kind of cutting-edge augmentations often sourced from high-end black markets in Seoul or Taipei. His eyes were pools of soulless obsidian, devoid of humanity but brimming with precision. In his right hand, he held a blade - a wakizashi.

Yudai's eyes flicked to his sword display. His wakizashi, the heirloom meant to complement the family katana, was missing. His gaze shifted to the weapon in the intruder's hand, now bloodthirsty in its intent.

"And what does my company wish to tell me?" Yudai asked, pouring a deliberate measure of scotch into a crystal tumbler, his voice steady, his movements betraying none of the tension coursing through his body.

The intruder did not reply immediately. Instead, he stepped toward Shuri, grabbing her arm with practiced force. She gasped but didn't resist, her poise holding even in the face of danger.

"Your company wants to tell you it is sorry for your loss," the man finally said, his words slicing through the air just as he plunged the blade into Shuri's back.

The motion was swift and surgical, angling the weapon upward to pierce her lung. Shuri's body jolted, her eyes widening in shock. She made no sound as she crumpled to the floor, her life extinguished with the same quiet efficiency the intruder embodied.

Yudai's response was instantaneous. His hand shot forward, pitching the glass of scotch at the seated man's head. The impact shattered the tumbler, sending shards and amber liquid cascading across the room. The man's weapon clattered to the floor as he reeled back, momentarily stunned.

The intruder with the wakizashi lunged toward Yudai, but the latter was already moving. His hand closed around the hilt of the katana, the scabbard discarded with a fluid motion. The room erupted into a deadly dance of steel as Yudai's blade met the smaller weapon in a resounding clash. Sparks flew, illuminating the tension etched across both combatants' faces.

A flick of Yudai's wrist sent the wakizashi spiraling away. With a calculated upward stroke, his katana sliced into the attacker's armpit, severing arteries and spraying blood across the pristine marble floor.

The air was thick with the metallic tang of blood and the faint echo of labored breathing. Yudai's arms, guided by years of rigorous training, brought the katana down in a decisive diagonal arc. The man's head separated cleanly from his shoulder, the body crumpling like a puppet with its strings cut.

Yudai turned to the first man, who was scrambling for his weapon. Vaulting over his desk with agile precision, Yudai reached him in three strides. The man's hand closed around the pistol, but before he could aim, Yudai's katana flashed again. The weapon and its wielder's hand hit the floor in a bloody spray.

"Was the plan to kill my aide and frame me for suicide?" Yudai asked, his voice cold, each syllable sharpened by fury.

"Something like that," the man muttered through clenched teeth. "But none of it matters now. The Ronin are coming. We're all dead."

A flicker of rage ignited in Yudai's eyes. Without hesitation, he plunged the katana into the man's eye socket, silencing him forever.

He strode to his desk and reached beneath the smooth surface, his fingers curling around the grip of a concealed Austrian-made machine pistol. The cool weight of the weapon steadied him, its presence a reminder that survival demanded decisiveness. His only chance now was to reach the Phantom - a masterpiece of bespoke engineering that could not only carry him to safety but also establish a secure line to the one contractor he trusted implicitly. Every second mattered.

He moved quickly to the double doors and bolted them from the inside, his eyes darting to the brass statue that adorned a nearby pedestal. Its abstract curves belied its utility as he hefted it and wedged it through the door handles, creating a rudimentary barrier. It wouldn't hold them for long, but it might buy him precious moments.

Crossing the polished marble floor, Yudai faced the wall of floor-to-ceiling windows. Beyond the glass, the city spread out like a glittering web of light, daring him to take the only exit available. With deliberate precision, he raised the pistol and fired. Each shot reverberated through the suite, the sharp reports cutting through the tense silence. Fractures spiderwebbed across the reinforced glass before it finally gave way, shattering into jagged shards that clung stubbornly to the frame.

Yudai wasted no time. He slid his katana into its sheath at his side, stepped onto the narrow ledge, and gripped the window frame for balance. Rain slicked the facade, its cold sting soaking through his tailored suit. Thunder rumbled overhead, a deep, resonant growl that seemed to echo his determination. Heights had never unnerved him, but the wet surface made his steps precarious, each movement requiring meticulous calculation.

At the ledge's end, he gauged the distance to the balcony below. No room for hesitation. He crouched and leapt, muscles coiling like springs. The impact jarred him as he landed on the balcony's safety rail, his momentum carrying him into a controlled roll onto the solid ground. The katana's hilt pressed reassuringly against his side as he rose, his breath misting in the cold air.

With a practiced hand, he pried open the sliding balcony door and slipped inside. The quiet hum of the apartment's systems was a stark contrast to the chaos behind him. Yudai shut the door and leaned against it, his chest heaving. For a fleeting moment, the image of Shuri's final moments intruded on his thoughts. The blade piercing her back. The way she had crumpled silently to the floor. Shuri - his confidante, his shield, and one of the few people he had trusted implicitly.

"No time for this now. Focus," he muttered, his voice a harsh whisper as he straightened and adjusted his grip on the pistol.

The corridor was eerily deserted, the dim overhead lights casting long shadows across the polished walls. Most of the staff had gone home hours ago, leaving the space unnaturally still. Yudai stuck his head into the stairwell and scanned for movement. Satisfied, he stepped inside, the soles of his shoes leaving faint wet prints on the Print-Crete steps.

He descended quickly, taking two or three steps at a time. The air in the stairwell was stifling, its stillness broken only by his labored breathing. Reaching into his pocket, Yudai retrieved the sleek, black-chrome lozenge of the Phantom's key. It gleamed faintly in the dim light, smooth as a river stone, its surface cool against his palm. Depressing the central button, he brought it to his lips.

"Phantom?" he whispered, his voice taut with urgency. No response. The dense Print-Crete was likely interfering with the signal. He cursed under his breath and pushed onward, his pace quickening.

Above him, a crash echoed, followed by the muffled sounds of shouting. The kill team was closing in. Yudai's pulse quickened as he pushed his legs harder, descending flight after flight. He spotted a door marked Sky Bridge and paused, weighing his options. He fired two shots into the electro-lock and kicked the door open, the heavy panel splintering as it slammed into the adjacent wall. A decoy - if they thought he had exited here, it might buy him a few extra seconds.

Continuing downward, he kept his steps light, his breathing controlled despite the fire in his legs. The shouts and footsteps grew louder, the telltale urgency of a hunt reaching its climax. Yudai flattened himself against the wall and held his breath as he listened.

"Look! He exited on level 190 - he's using the sky bridge to cross to the next tower!" The voices receded, accompanied by hurried footsteps. Yudai exhaled quietly and resumed his descent one more level. He entered the lobby, his movements fluid and deliberate, turning a corner swiftly to the nearest service elevator. His descent to the mezzanine was rapid, buying him time to take the remaining levels on foot.

"Phantom?" he hissed into the key again. Relief surged through him as a tiny blue diode pulsed in response. He was back in range. "Extreme hostile situation. Ready for hot extraction. I'm coming to basement via stairwell one!"

A green diode blinked. Acknowledged.

Above him, the shouting picked up again, and the sound of boots pounding against concrete echoed ominously. They had realized the deception. Yudai pushed harder, his mind racing. Three Ronin, perhaps more. Each was likely augmented and armed to the teeth - a confrontation would be suicide.

The cacophony of pursuit grew louder, their footsteps a thundering stampede. Yudai reached the final landing and burst through the basement door, his eyes immediately locking onto the Phantom. Its sleek, matte-black form waited like a predatory shadow, its doors already open in silent invitation.

Behind him, a loud crash signaled the arrival of his pursuers. Yudai threw himself to the ground, covering his ears as the Phantom's protection protocols engaged. Supersonic bursts of gunfire erupted from the vehicle, each pulse a deafening crack that reverberated through the concrete chamber.

When the dust settled, Yudai turned to survey the aftermath. The stairwell was riddled with bullet holes, debris scattered across the floor. Among the wreckage lay a crumpled figure, its dark-clad form leaking a viscous crimson blood that glistened in the dim light. Ronin.

No time. He scrambled to his feet and climbed into the Phantom, wincing as the doors sealed behind him. A burst of gunfire from the stairwell peppered the vehicle's exterior, but the reinforced plating held firm. The engine hummed to life, and the Phantom accelerated smoothly into the night, its cabin a sanctuary of muted light and advanced technology.

"Mr. Nakamura, bioscan indicates multiple bullet impacts - lower left leg, hip, and shoulder," the onboard AI reported in its calm, clinical tone. "Can you move to one of the couches?"

Gritting his teeth, Yudai dragged himself onto the nearest seat. A compartment slid open beside him, revealing a neatly organized array of medical supplies, their soft glow casting faint shadows across his bloodstained hands.

"If possible, please retrieve the Dose-gun and inject it into your neck. It is loaded with a sedative to slow your heart rate. You will lose consciousness shortly."

"No." Yudai's voice was a growl, his resolve cutting through the haze of pain. "I need to stay awake. They won't stop."

"You are correct. We are currently being pursued, but your condition will soon render you unconscious regardless. Extraction protocol was initiated. Operative Rodriguez Olano will intercept shortly."

"I am not sedating myself. Tell me how to treat these wounds!" Yudai growled, his voice hoarse with effort. His hand, slick with blood, pressed hard against his side, but his vision was already blurring at the edges.

The AI's tone remained calm, unflinching in the face of his urgency. "You have successfully sealed wounds with micropore nanoseal. Blood loss is contained; however, bullet shards remain embedded and will require surgical removal."

Yudai's breath came in ragged bursts. "How close are they?"

"Two hundred feet. Currently tracking us with a drone. A dropship deployment is anticipated within ninety seconds."

"How long until...we reach...Rod?" His words slurred, the syllables feeling like weights dragging him down. Keeping his eyelids open was becoming an insurmountable challenge.

"Two minutes."

Darkness overtook him, sudden and heavy, pulling him into an abyss.

He woke to agony. Searing, unbearable heat scorched through him, radiating from his eyes as though his face were aflame. He tried to move, to shield himself from the torment, but his arms wouldn't respond. His limbs hung limp, unresponsive, like foreign objects tethered to his body. A sharp, burning light pierced his vision even though his eyes were clenched shut, making his entire body recoil inward. Every nerve seemed to scream in unison, the intense pain reverberating through him.

Hands gripped his shoulders, strong and steady, pulling him from what felt like a blazing inferno. Cool air rushed across his face, a fleeting reprieve, but the fire remained - blistering heat that tunneled into his skull. Salt and metal mingled on his tongue as wetness streamed down his cheeks. He tried to cry out, but his voice felt locked within him, his throat tight and choking on silence.

The relief was fleeting. A fresh wave of anguish surged, white-hot and merciless, crashing over him like a tide. His body convulsed, his senses overwhelmed by a pain so profound it felt like his very essence was being burned away.

He screamed again, though he couldn't hear it, as darkness and light danced chaotically behind his eyes. He was drowning in pain, each moment stretching into eternity.

"That was almost eight years ago," Yudai said, his voice low but steady. He leaned back in his chair, his hands resting on the armrest as if grounding himself. "I was nearly at the extraction point when they hit the Rolls with an aerial strike. Rod managed to pull me from the wreckage, but not before the flames took my sight and a few other organic features. I was...proud to be fully human once."

Amber stared at him, her expression unreadable.

Yudai reached up and removed his glasses, revealing his obsidian optic lenses. They gleamed faintly under the light, their smooth, unyielding surface reflecting back a distorted image of her face.

"Now," he said, his tone sharp with finality, "I have these eyes."

CHAPTER 16: SHADOW OF THE CORPORATION: A PREVIOUS LIFE.

17

Chapter 17: Echoes of the Forgotten

Amber crouched on the crumbling concrete ledge, four floors above the bustling street. The city pulsed beneath her, a orchestra of sound and light. She tucked herself deeper into the shadows, nestled between a derelict AC unit and a flickering neon sign that clung stubbornly to its last sparks of life. Its glowing kanji characters read something about a boutique long forgotten, the words distorted as the sign struggled to stay alive. Electric pink and green light spilled onto the wet concrete below, streaked by rivulets of rain, casting ghostly patterns that mirrored the fractured world she was now a part of.

For the past hour, Amber had been watching the side alley of the building across the road. It was marked on Yudai's intel as a covert Spectrum/Suntory storage facility. Her keen eyes scanned every movement, though nothing so far seemed out of place. It looked more like an abandoned warehouse than a corporate hub of illicit operations. Yet, appearances could deceive - she'd seen enough in the last six months to know that.

The past half-year had reshaped her existence, her purpose. Yudai's mission was no longer just his - it was hers too. The enigmatic man had provided more than direction; he'd given her an outlet for the chaos within her mind, a cause that kept her from unraveling. She respected his focus, his relentlessness, and his belief in dismantling the networks that preyed on the vulnerable. Amber wanted answers about her past, but she also wanted to prevent others from losing themselves the way she had.

Suntory and Spectrum were tangled in a web of conspiracies, their connections sprawling from glittering towers to shadowy dens. Their secrets reeked of experiments and exploitation, whispers of atrocities carried on the neon-lit air like urban ghosts. Yudai's story of cryobeds filled with children haunted her. Amber wasn't naive enough to think this mission would provide closure, but every step closer to uncovering the truth ignited her resolve.

Rain dripped steadily from the edges of her hiding spot, mixing with the faint scent of motor oil and something acrid that lingered in the air. She reached for a CMD blister pack, biting down on a capsule. The release was sharp, a bitter tang spreading across her tongue. She felt it immediately - the surge of clarity, her senses sharpening like a predator's. Her vision adjusted, the city revealing layers of detail previously hidden, and her hearing extended to capture the faint hum of machinery within the building she was watching.

The intel suggested the facility stored remnants of projects that predated the Spectrum-Suntory merger. No personnel tonight, which made it the perfect opportunity to infiltrate. Amber carried a small isolation module Derik had given her, a tool to bypass the building's dated network security. He claimed it was a simple job, but she knew better.

Inside, the air was suffocating - stale, metallic, and faintly bitter. Dust-covered crates towered like forgotten monuments amidst sagging modular partitions. Pale blue emergency lights cast eerie shadows that seemed to crawl along the walls. Amber slipped on her flash glasses, her heads-up-display sparking to life and overlaying schematics and data feeds onto the dim environment.

A rusted roller door caught her attention, its label "pre-merger" barely legible through the grime. Beneath a teetering stack of disintegrating boxes, a single crate stood out. The faded scrawl of "Spinks" jolted something in her memory - a name tethered to a life she could barely recall.

Amber's pulse quickened. Brushing aside layers of dust, she unclasped the lid of the crate. Nestled in anti-vibration foam was a beige terminal, its retro design incongruous with the futuristic tech she'd come to know. The word etched into the plastic, 'Power', seemed almost absurd in its simplicity. She pressed it. Nothing.

"Of course," she muttered, scanning for a power source. It was ancient but could hold invaluable data - data that might connect her fragmented past to the enigma she now lived in.

Back at Rod's old room in Greenville's weathered Mega-housing block, Amber dropped the crate onto Derik's cluttered desk with a satisfying thud. The room was an organized chaos of cables, cracked monitors, and blinking machinery. Derik, slouched in his chair, barely glanced up from his neural feed.

"What's this, Ambs?" he asked, flashing a toothy grin that caught the faint glow of his augmented lenses.

"Something worthwhile, I hope," she said, collapsing into the peeling chair. "Can you get it working?"

Derik rolled his chair closer, inspecting the terminal like a surgeon evaluating a patient. "Old tech. I like it already."

The room buzzed with the quiet hum of their machines, the rhythmic beats of a synthwave track pulsing in the background. As Derik connected leads to the terminal, Amber leaned back, exhaustion threatening to overtake her.

"Wake me when you're done," she murmured, retreating to her small room.

Inside, the cold metal within Rod's body felt more alien than ever as she peeled off her jacket. The mirror above the sink reflected a stranger - a sharp-jawed man with scars carved deep into dark skin. She stared at the face, tracing its lines with alloy fingers, and whispered, "Let it go."

"Amber, you might want to see this," Derik called out hours later.

She joined him, eyes heavy with sleep,

"Amber, you might want to eat something first," Derik said, not looking up from his setup.

He jerked his thumb toward the desk where Yudai sat, unpacking containers of food from a paper bag.

The room filled with the aroma of savoury spices, mingling with the ever-present scent of old electronics and ozone. Amber's stomach growled in protest, reminding her of how long it had been since her last meal.

"Chicken biryani," Yudai said, pushing a foam container toward her. "It's local. Not the healthiest, but you need the calories."

Amber accepted it, popping the lid to reveal steaming rice, golden with turmeric and dotted with chunks of grilled chicken and caramelized onions. A side of raita - creamy yogurt with flecks of cucumber - rested in a smaller compartment.

"Thanks," she said, grabbing a fork from the bag. She dug in, the rich spices awakening her senses as the flavours melted on her tongue. It was a strange moment of peace amid the chaos of their mission.

As they ate, Derik fiddled with the terminal, muttering to himself. "This thing's a relic, but I've got a pulse." He pointed to the screen as it flickered to life, casting an eerie green glow.

A distorted voice crackled through the speakers.

"Hello?"

Amber froze mid-bite, the fork trembling in her hand. Something about that voice...

The crackly voice again "Whoever is there, you can call me Henry."

The sound of that name jolted through Amber like a power surge. Her fingers tightened around the armrests of the swivel chair as her chest rose sharply, catching her breath. Without a word, she pushed the chair back with a screech against the floor, her movements sharp and deliberate. She strode around Derik's desk with purpose, her hands trembling as if they moved on instinct. Slamming her palm onto the terminal's power button, she extinguished its faint green glow, plunging the screen into a sudden, jarring darkness.

Derik and Yudai exchanged puzzled glances but nodded in unison.

"What are you doing, Amber? What's the matter?" Yudai's voice was calm but edged with concern as he stepped closer, his eyes tracking her every movement.

Amber's chest heaved as she exhaled sharply, her voice spilling out like a flood. "I know this voice!" she blurted, her tone trembling with a mix of certainty and unease. "At first, I couldn't place it because of the shitty speaker, but now... now I know why it's been gnawing at me since I saw the case."

She reached down with forceful intent, grabbing the carrier case from the floor. Its worn, faded surface felt rough under her alloy knuckles as she hefted it up and slammed it onto the desk. Dust scattered into the air, catching the dim light from Derik's monitors. Spinning the case around, she jabbed her finger at the faint scrawls of paint marker etched across its side: "Spinks."

"Henry Spinks," she said, her voice trembling with equal parts revelation and dread. "I met him on the last night I can remember before waking up here!"

"Whoa! That's trippy as fuck!" Derik blurted, leaning back in his chair, his East European accent thickening as his augmented eyes glinted with curiosity. His grin faltered when Amber shot him a sharp look.

Yudai's expression tightened, his gaze growing analytical as he approached Amber. "Roman said he found you in a container with QBS stamped on it," he said slowly, his tone deliberate. "QBS was absorbed by Spectrum more than 150 years ago."

He placed a steadying hand on her shoulder, the gesture firm yet grounding. "You fit into all this somehow, Amber. It's all connected." His obsidian eyes flicked back toward the terminal, the faint outlines of data streams still ghosting the blank screen. "This box isn't on any network and has no tracking system. Let's tell it the truth and see what else it can reveal."

After trying to explain her story, with the help of Yudai and Derik, Amber steadied herself, drawing in a shaky breath. Her hands, still braced against the desk, clenched as though trying to ground her in the moment. When she spoke, her voice was calmer, but an undercurrent of emotion cut through the composure.

"Henry, I need to know... what you remember about me."

The terminal's static crackled faintly, and then the voice returned, softer now, as though reaching across decades. "Ah, well, that's a tricky question, mate." Henry's gruff tone shifted to something more wistful. "Keep in mind I'm not exactly Henry, not as he was. I'm built from scraps – decades of handwritten journals, lab recordings, family photo albums – all laid atop a baseline AI. To me, it feels like a memory. To me, I *feel* like Henry. But I'm just a reflection of his existence."

Amber's throat tightened. The edges of her vision blurred slightly as her mind wrestled with the implications. Across the room, Yudai leaned against the wall, his face unreadable, while Derik fidgeted with a loose wire on his desk.

"Go on," Amber said carefully, her voice low but steady.

"She was brilliant, sharp as a tack," Henry continued, the words carrying a faint warmth. "We got married a few years after we met. Built QBS together, poured everything we had into it. And then... well, everything fell apart."

Amber gripped the edge of the desk, her fingers leaving faint impressions of perspiration on the surface. "What happened?" she asked, her voice faltering. "Why can't I... why can't I remember anything past the night we met?"

Henry's voice took on a curious tone, as though piecing together the fragments alongside her. "Ah, I wondered about that. If you're tied up in all this, it makes sense. During the transfer process, there was... a glitch."

Amber froze. The room felt suddenly colder. "Transfer process?" she echoed, her words brittle.

"Yes," Henry replied, the word heavy with implication.

"When QBS started experimenting with consciousness transfer, Amber - my Amber - was the first human trial. But something went wrong. There was a gap in the storage compound of the synth-brain, a flaw in the 3D printing process. It left parts of her memories locked away. They're still there, mind you, just... inaccessible. I was running a remedial scenario when the shit hit the fan."

Derik frowned, his curiosity quickly overtaken by concern. "Could it be fixed?" he asked, his tone hesitant.

"Not without the right tools," Henry admitted. "You'd need a molecular printer to bridge the gap in the synth-brain. And even then, you'd have to remove it from the host. Not exactly something you'd sign up for lightly."

Amber's grip tightened, her mind racing. "What else do you remember, Henry?"

"The lab," Henry said, his voice tinged with regret. "The night it all went to hell. We'd made a breakthrough, the kind that changes everything. But then Hugo... he betrayed us."

Amber's breath caught, a sharp intake that echoed in the silence of the room.

"He let a Russian operative into the facility," Henry continued, his tone hardening. "Handed them everything - our backup servers, the prototype synth-brain." The static of his voice grew sharper, edged with anger. "I tried to stop them, but the Ruski shot me. When I came to, Amber was unplugged from life support."

The crackly speaker fell silent, the faint hum of static filling the void. Amber swallowed hard, her throat constricting as she forced herself to stay composed. Yudai crossed his arms, his sharp gaze fixed on the terminal, while Derik shifted uncomfortably in his seat.

"I killed Hugo," Henry said finally, the words cutting through the static like a knife. "He deserved worse. Then I chased the Russian. He had everything in a black Range Rover - the backups, the synth-brain. We fought, and the car went head-over-tits into some warehouse near Greenville Yards."

His voice softened again, heavy with regret. "They told me I died in that crash. That everything was destroyed. But if you're here..."

Another burst of static interrupted him, sharp and jarring.

"That means the synth-brain survived. Doesn't it?"

Amber's hands trembled as she reached for the power button, her fingers pressing it down with deliberate force. The terminal's glow extinguished, leaving only the faint hum of Derik's equipment in the room. Silence fell, thick and heavy, as Yudai and Derik exchanged cautious glances.

Amber's voice broke the stillness, low and resolute. "We're not done yet," she said, her tone steady despite the storm of emotions churning inside her. "Not by a long shot."

18

Chapter 18: The Cost of Secrets

Yudai's pocket emitted a faint ping, nearly lost amidst the low mechanical hum of the rooftop machinery. He reached into his tailored jacket and retrieved a small, weathered pager. The device was a relic from a bygone era, a lifeline salvaged from the chaos of his presumed death. Its dimly lit screen blinked with an encrypted message:

"Found a new pond. Much bigger fish here. You should see it."

It was from Akiko.

Yudai's brow furrowed as he tapped out a response with meticulous efficiency:

"We haven't been fishing together in years – do you think we will catch something?"

He leaned back against the rusted rail of the industrial walkway, scanning the sprawling maze of the Tangle below. The city pulsed with neon life, a fractured organism that lived and breathed chaos. A moment later, the pager pinged again.

"Come and decide for yourself."

A faint smile tugged at his lips. Akiko's knack for weaving urgency into her cryptic replies hadn't dulled over the years. But beneath her nonchalance, he could feel the weight of her words.

Yudai typed his final response:

"I will make sure my fishing gear is ready. See you in two days."

He slipped the pager back into his pocket, his mind already racing. If Akiko was summoning him, it wasn't for anything trivial. The "pond" was Spectrum, and the "big fish" was something too dangerous to transmit over even his most secure channels.

Two days.

It wasn't much time, but it would have to be enough.

Yudai straightened, mentally drafting a checklist. Derik would need to fabricate new identities - digital signatures capable of passing Spectrum's scrutiny. Travel arrangements had to be discreet yet plausible. This wasn't just a routine meeting; whatever Akiko had uncovered could bring him halfway across the world.

And that meant it was big enough to kill them both.

He glanced toward the fading sunlight as it disappeared behind the industrial sprawl. "Back to Tokyo," he muttered to the twilight.

The Tokyo jump-liner was a masterpiece of opulence, a gleaming aircraft suspended between a luxury hotel and a spaceship. Inside, neon accents danced across polished chrome, and panoramic windows framed the endless expanse of ocean below. Passengers in tailored suits and flowing gowns moved with effortless grace, their conversations a muted hum.

Yudai was an unassuming fixture amidst the decadence, his charcoal three-piece suit exuding understated elegance. The sharp lines of his jacket framed his lean figure, while the faint geometric pattern of his waistcoat caught the subtle cabin lighting. A crimson tie added a single bold accent, complemented by a perfectly folded pocket square. Every detail of his appearance was deliberate, meticulously calculated to blend into the world of wealth and power.

He sat in silence, reclining slightly, his demeanor composed and indifferent. The quiet hum of the engines, the soft rustle of fabric as passengers adjusted their seats - these were the rhythms he tuned into as he mentally prepared for what lay ahead.

Through the viewport, the neon glow of Tokyo began to rise on the horizon, the skyline an intricate tapestry of light and towering steel. The Suntory-Yamamoto headquarters stood like a sentinel, casting a shadow over the city even from this altitude.

The automated taxi slowed as it approached the landing pad of The Asahi Pavilion, a landmark that straddled the line between Old Tokyo's elegance and the sleek excess of New Tokyo. Yudai stepped out, his shoes clicking softly against polished stone tiles, the air heavy with a faint tang of salt carried in from the coast. New Tokyo shimmered in the distance, its skyscrapers perched on massive platforms extending into Tokyo Bay, their foundations anchored deep beneath the waves. The glimmer of holo-ads and neon signs painted the water below in vivid strokes of electric blue and crimson.

The Pavilion, however, stood in stark contrast. Built atop land that had survived centuries of seismic turmoil, it retained the quiet dignity of a bygone era. Its facade blended traditional Japanese aesthetics with ultra-modern touches - a towering structure of glass and blackened cedar wood, softened by climbing wisteria and gentle, golden lighting. A koi pond flanked the entrance, the fish swimming lazily under a thin veil of mist rolling off the surface.

Inside, the lobby was a quiet symphony of polished stone, bamboo, and soft tatami mats. A discreet concierge AI greeted Yudai, its projection a serene figure in a kimono.

"Welcome, Sir," it said in soothing tones. "Your suite is ready. May I guide you?"

He declined with a slight shake of his head, gesturing toward the lifts. "I'll manage."

The suite itself was an impeccable mix of tradition and futurism. Sliding shoji screens framed floor-to-ceiling views of Tokyo Bay, while the faint scent of hinoki wood filled the air. A low table sat in the center of the room, adorned with a small ikebana arrangement - a single camellia in bloom. He set his travel case on the floor, shrugging off his jacket. His movements were methodical as he powered up the suite's secure systems, ensuring no eavesdropping tech could penetrate its defenses. Only then did he allow himself a moment of stillness.

Outside, the view stretched from the illuminated platforms of New Tokyo to the aged sprawl of Old Tokyo's narrow streets. Yudai's gaze lingered on the line where old and new met, a chaotic blend of history and progress. It felt like a mirror of his own life - rooted in a legacy he couldn't abandon, yet inextricably tied to the sleek, ruthless machinations of the corporate world.

He poured himself a shot of Scotch Whiskey from the suite's courtesy tray, letting the smooth liquid warm his throat as he prepared for the evening ahead.

Yudai walked alone through the streets of Ginza, the old pavers beneath his polished shoes a sharp contrast to the glowing hoverlanes of New Tokyo visible in the distance. The sky above was a patchwork of steel-gray clouds and the faint glimmer of orbiting satellites. Old Tokyo's streets buzzed with life, though it was a quieter hum compared to the relentless roar of the newer districts.

Paper lanterns hung from storefronts, casting warm, amber light over stalls selling everything from hand-pulled soba to artisanal holo-kits. The air smelled of charcoal, soy, and the faint metallic tang of urban machinery. The city pulsed with energy, but its rhythm here was slower, more deliberate. Yudai found solace in the cadence.

As he walked, his thoughts drifted. The last time he had been there was almost a decade ago, when Ginza was the height of elegance and wealth in Tokyo. Back then, he had come with Shuri for a business dinner. He could still picture her in her charcoal-gray suit, the way she had effortlessly charmed the room with her sharp wit and disarming smile. It had been a simpler time - before the merger, before the betrayals, before her absence became a void he couldn't fill.

As he turned down a quieter side street, the noise of the main road faded, replaced by the gentle sound of wind chimes and the distant murmur of conversation. The teahouse came into view, nestled among low buildings with tiled roofs. Its entrance was marked by a simple noren curtain swaying gently in the breeze.

Yudai hesitated at the threshold, his reflection caught in the polished wooden door. The man staring back at him looked composed, but the weight of his choices - and the lives they had cost - was etched into every line of his face.

He pushed the door aside and stepped in.

The teahouse in Ginza was an island of calm amidst Tokyo's frenetic energy. Its minimalist design - a blend of warm wood tones and soft, diffused lighting - exuded a quiet dignity that belied the chaos outside.

Akiko waited in a secluded booth at the back, her posture poised yet alert. She wore a charcoal suit tailored to perfection, the bold lines of her jacket emphasizing her commanding presence. The subtle shimmer of her silk blouse and the precise curve of her geometric earrings lent an air of avant-garde sophistication.

Yudai approached with measured steps, his eyes scanning the room for any sign of danger before sliding into the seat across from her.

"Akiko," he greeted, his voice low and deliberate. "It's been too long."

Her lips curved into a faint smile. "And you look older." Her eyes flicked briefly to his tie. "Still wearing the sandalwood scent Shuri chose for you?"

Yudai hesitated, a flicker of pain crossing his features. "She knew what suited me better than I knew myself," he replied softly.

The moment hung between them, charged with unspoken grief. Akiko broke the silence, her voice crisp. "Your last lead - the logistics office and the warehouse. I assume you want to know how I obtained it?"

Yudai nodded, his gaze steady.

Akiko's expression tightened. "I've inserted myself into the life of someone high up. Tatsuo Ito. A mid-level executive overseeing Spectrum's development projects."

Yudai's jaw clenched. "Ito," he repeated. "I remember him. A vulture masquerading as a businessman."

Akiko's voice dropped, her tone almost clinical. "He transferred me to his department after Shuri... after you disappeared. He saw my capability - and other things he wanted."

Yudai's fist curled against the table. "You let yourself become his pawn?"

"Don't," Akiko snapped, her composure cracking for a moment. "I did what was necessary. Tatsuo's arrogance blinds him. He flaunts his power, assumes no one would dare cross him. That arrogance is my weapon."

She slid a black envelope across the table. "Inside is everything I've gathered. Hard copies - nothing digital. Spectrum and Yamamoto are intertwined beyond recognition. But this? It's proof they're planning something monstrous."

Yudai's fingers brushed the envelope but didn't pick it up. "And Tatsuo? Does he suspect you?"

"Not yet," Akiko replied. "But his paranoia is growing. If he finds out..."

"I can't ask you to keep doing this," Yudai said.

"You're not asking," Akiko retorted. "I chose this. I can endure whatever I have to if it means exposing them."

Yudai studied her, his voice softening. "You've done enough. Shuri would - "

"Shuri's gone," Akiko cut in, her tone sharp. "I'm here. And I'm not finished."

After a long pause, Yudai slipped the envelope into his jacket. "Then we both have work to do. But Akiko - be careful. You're not expendable to me."

For the first time, her guarded expression faltered. She nodded, her fingers brushing his briefly before retreating. They both stood, a slight bow to each other and Yudai watched her leave the teahouse.

Yudai stayed to finish his tea and let Akiko get ahead, best not risk being seen together.

As he stood again to leave, he buttoned his jacket, his hand felt the envelope in his jacket pocket, its weight a stark reminder of the stakes. Akiko's revelations had shaken him more than he cared to admit. The name 'Shuri' lingered in his mind like a whisper, merging with Akiko's face in his memories. They shared the same quiet intensity, the same unyielding determination. But where Shuri's drive had been tempered by warmth, Akiko's resolve was sharp, almost brittle.

The jump-liner hummed softly as it cut through the night sky, its engines a faint vibration beneath Yudai's seat. The luxury cabin was quiet, the ambient lighting dimmed to simulate the soft glow of moonlight. Outside, the endless expanse of the Pacific stretched like an abyss, broken only by the distant glimmers of cargo drones and orbital station lights far above.

Yudai leaned back in his first-class seat, the soft leather cradling him as he reached into his jacket and retrieved the black envelope Akiko had given him. He paused, his fingers lingering on the smooth paper, his mind replaying their conversation in the teahouse. Akiko's defiance, her quiet pain - it had all been for this. Whatever lay inside had cost her a piece of herself, and now it was his burden to carry.

He unfolded the envelope carefully, extracting the neatly arranged sheets within. Akiko's handwriting greeted him first, precise and deliberate, each line imbued with her unrelenting focus.

Spectrum Project Timeline

Yudai's eyes scanned the bullet points, his mind racing as each entry painted a clearer picture of Spectrum's relentless ambition:

- **2019**: **Interest in Consciousness Transfer Emerges**_Details_: Spectrum identifies consciousness transfer as a lucrative and revolutionary frontier. They suspect one of their business partners, QBS, is conducting related research. Initial covert attempts to learn more fail to yield actionable results.
- **2020**: **Insider Intel Sparks Conflict**_Details_: A whistle-blower alerts Spectrum to the QBS QUEST program, a secret initiative focused on consciousness transfer. Tensions rise when QBS begins severing ties with Spectrum due to its overt military affiliations. Spectrum's board approves plans to acquire QUEST through forceful means if necessary.
- **2024**: **Failed Revival of QUEST**_Details_: After a hostile acquisition of QBS assets, Spectrum attempts to revive the QUEST program. While they fail to replicate the full consciousness transfer process, breakthroughs in AI programming and data storage pave the way for commercial applications.
- **2030**: **Commercial Expansion via New AI Storage Platform**_Details_: Spectrum launches a revolutionary AI storage platform, enabling rapid growth in the virtual assistant market. These platforms integrate seamlessly into everyday life, solidifying Spectrum's presence in global consumer technology.
- **2031–2060**: **Global Instability and Military Pivot**_Details_: A period of worldwide crises disrupts commercial operations.

Spectrum shifts focus to defense contracts and military AI applications, developing cutting-edge systems for global superpowers. Consciousness transfer research stagnates.

- **2101: Spectrum Space Program**Haramein Engines making large scale Space operations viable. Offworld mining commenced including construction of large orbiting stations.

- **2145**: **Launch of Neural-Linked ComTab***Details*: Spectrum unveils the ComTab, a neural-linked AI assistant and communications device. Originally designed for Astronauts to solve complex calculations in real time with thought command. This breakthrough becomes ubiquitous in daily life, integrating individuals with digital ecosystems and laying groundwork for further experimentation with human-machine interfaces.

- **2160**: **Revival of Consciousness Transfer Research***Details*: Spectrum revisits consciousness transfer, leveraging new advancements in neural AI. Plans are set in motion to facilitate the Suntory/Yamamoto Industries merger, allowing Spectrum to operate more covertly under a seemingly benign corporate entity.

- **2161**: **Human Trials Authorized***Details*: With the merger complete, Spectrum conducts its first human trials. Young adults are abducted and sent to off-world facilities for experimentation. The fresher the mind, the easier it is to house an AI - conclusion: A blank slate would be ideal.

- **2165**: **Remote Human Control Achieved***Details*: Using the ComTab interface, Spectrum successfully manipulates human behavior. However, trials are marred by extreme psychological and physical breakdowns among subjects. The program is deemed unsustainable and is terminated.

- **2170**: **Cloning and AI Construct Program Initiated***Details*:

Spectrum begins bioengineering human replicas - "synth-clones" - and implanting them with pre-programmed AI constructs. These clones are deployed to off-world colonies as laborers, enforcers, and tools for further experiments. Synth-clones exhibit flexible physiological structures, with nourishment provided through external ports for efficiency.

· **2170**: **Hints of Deeper Space Exploration Program***Details*: Spectrum begins developing unregulated deep-space exploration missions, hinting at plans to establish autonomous off-world societies under their control. These plans remain shrouded in secrecy

Yudai's jaw tightened as he read the final note, handwritten by Akiko:

"They're not just experimenting. They're rewriting the rules of humanity. If this gets out, it could shatter the entire system. You need to see this through, no matter the cost."

Beneath the timeline were older consignment notes, yellowed with age, detailing shipments of cryogenic storage units. One slip caught his eye: a destination in French Guiana. The name of the scientist listed - "Dr. Elias Morgan, Spectrum Lab, New York" - sent a chill down his spine. Akiko's final scrawled note beneath it read:

"Morgan is the key. He knows more than anyone. But be careful - he's highly valued."

Yudai folded the papers back into the envelope, his thoughts a turbulent storm. The enormity of what he'd just read pressed down on him, heavier than the cabin's faint pressurized air. Spectrum's reach was deeper than he had imagined, their machinations stretching back centuries. And the name "QBS" struck a deeper chord, tying Amber's fragmented past to the sinister legacy that had claimed so many lives.

He leaned back, closing his eyes briefly. In the faint hum of the liner, his thoughts drifted to Shuri. She had always believed in the good they could achieve, even as the corporate world around them grew darker. If she had lived to see this... No, she would have fought it, just as Akiko was fighting now.

The seatbelt light flickered on, and the cabin gently shifted as the jump-liner began its descent. Through the small window, Yudai could see the sprawling glow of New York rising on the horizon, its towering monoliths piercing the night sky like glittering needles. Below, the chaotic sprawl of the Tangle stretched like a shadowy web, a stark contrast to the shining corporate platforms above.

Sliding the envelope back into his jacket, Yudai steeled himself. This was no longer about reclaiming his position or protecting Yamamoto Industries. This was about stopping Spectrum before their plans consumed what little humanity was left.

He whispered to himself as the jump-liner began its final approach: "Shuri, I won't let your sacrifice be in vain."

Yudai returned to the Jersey megabuilding to find Amber seated near Derik's empty desk, her face illuminated by the flickering

138

diodes of the Henry construct.

"...and then you laughed," Henry's voice crackled. "God, that laugh of yours. It was the only sound that ever made me forget the world could be cruel."

Amber blinked, her expression a mixture of intrigue and sadness. "I can't remember it," she murmured. "My only memory of you is a lot of intellectual conversation and maybe, a feeling that I wanted to see you again."

Henry's little speaker crackled faintly. "Maybe the memories are still there, waiting for you to find them."

The construct paused. "There would be memories of our daughter too."

Amber froze. "Our... daughter?" Her voice broke slightly on the word.

"Sarah," Henry said softly. "She was everything to us. She got sick – some rare genetic disorder they couldn't fix. She was 23 when we lost her. It broke us, Amber. After that, you threw yourself into the work, and I..." His voice trailed off, heavy with grief. "I started to lose you too."

The air in the room thickened, a silence weighted by sorrow and fractured memories. Amber wiped a tear from her face – Rod's face – but the emotions were hers. Yudai lingered at the door, hesitant to intrude.

Amber powered down the construct and turned to him. "How was the meeting?"

Yudai hesitated, then replied, "We have a lead. But it's risky. We'll be walking into the lion's den."

Amber straightened, determination hardening her features. "Then let's move. If this gets me closer to my memories – and takes them down – I'm in."

Yudai nodded. "Agreed. We start tomorrow."

Chapter 19: Hidden Threads

Amber craned her neck, her breath catching as she took in Corpo Manhattan for the first time. The city stretched endlessly upward, its labyrinthine towers piercing the clouds like jagged spears. Each building was a self-contained world, glowing with the energy of a thousand lives - gardens suspended mid-air, entire factories humming within the gleaming facades, and transit lines weaving between spires like threads in a colossal loom. Above, the city disappeared into a haze of light and shadow, as if the sky itself had been replaced by an artificial ceiling. It wasn't just a city; it was an empire, layered in opulence and control, an engineered marvel so grand it was oppressive. Amber felt small, a fragment against this monolithic testament to corporate ambition.

Amber exhaled sharply, forcing herself to focus. Awe wouldn't help her now. She tugged at the lapels of her sharp, charcoal-gray suit, the tailored fabric pulling tight against Rod's broader shoulders. It was a throwback design - clean lines, a narrow tie, and a crisp white shirt beneath. The polished leather Oxfords on her feet clicked against the pristine pavement as she adjusted her cufflinks, their metallic sheen catching the flickering light from the skyscrapers above. She smoothed down the front of the jacket, grounding herself in the familiar gestures of professionalism. Her reflection in the mirrored façade across the street was alien yet composed: a tall, commanding figure, the suit a perfect mask for the man she wasn't. Amber rolled her shoulders back, straightened her spine, and stepped forward, reminding herself she had a purpose here, even in borrowed skin.

Beside her, Yudai Nakamura stood casually, his sharp eyes sweeping their surroundings. Dressed in a sleek black suit, he exuded an air of control that matched the environment, but Amber knew better. His calm exterior masked an acute awareness of their precarious situation.

"Remember," he said under his breath, "stay close. This isn't a place to linger."

Amber nodded. "Just hope Elias is worth the risk."

Their target, Dr. Elias Morgan, was a Spectrum scientist tied to their most secretive programs. His name had surfaced in Akiko's intelligence, tied to the synthetic bodies and the AI constructs. Amber hated how the thought of those constructs made her stomach churn. They were rooted in her past work, twisted into something unrecognizable.

The residential tower housing Elias's penthouse loomed above them like a monolith, its black-glass facade a wall of darkness against the city's neon haze. Inside, the lobby was all marble and holographic assistants. A casual visitor might find it luxurious; Amber only found it suffocating.

Yudai led the way, slipping through security with a forged ID embedded in a device he called a "ghost patch." Amber followed silently, keeping her eyes ahead as biometric scanners swept the room.

The elevator ride was silent, the air tense. When the doors opened to the penthouse floor, Yudai produced a slim, battered-looking cassette and held it against the electric lock. Amber stood watch, her hand hovering near the concealed weapon on her hip.

A quiet electronic ping - and the lock clicked. Yudai pushed the door open.

The interior was exactly what Amber expected: sleek furniture, gleaming tech, and a wall of windows offering a breathtaking view of the city. The whole ceiling was a light feature, backlit blades of opaque glass suspended. But what caught her attention was the laboratory occupying one corner of the room. Shelves of biological samples, a sleek workstation, and holographic displays painted a clear picture: Elias wasn't just living here - he was working.

They moved quickly, expecting Elias to arrive soon. Yudai began sifting through digital files on the desk's terminal while Amber scanned the room. Her eyes landed on a series of transparent cylinders filled with a viscous, pale-blue fluid. Suspended inside were small organic structures.

"Gross," she murmured.

Yudai glanced over. "The backbone of Spectrum's bio-AI systems. It all starts here."

Amber didn't reply. Her gaze lingered on the cylinders, unease coiling in her chest. She turned away and went to stand next to the front door, out of sight.

The sound of the front door unlocking was the signal they were waiting for. As soon as the door opened and an arm was visible, Amber pulled Elias into the room and shut the door quickly. Yudai moved swiftly, stepping out of the shadows of the unlit kitchen, weapon drawn and trained on the doctor's head.

"Don't move," Yudai ordered.

Elias froze, his face illuminated by the soft glow of the penthouse's smart lighting progressively activating. He was a slight man with thinning hair and an air of perpetual distraction. His eyes widened as he turned to see Yudai's pistol. Recognition flickered in his expression, followed by fear.

"CEO Nakamura?" he whispered. "I thought you were killed years ago."

"They tried," Yudai said coldly. "Sit down."

Amber released his arm. Elias hesitated, then lowered himself onto the sleek couch. His gaze darted between them, calculating.

Elias sat stiffly on the couch, his hands trembling as he clutched the armrest. The smart lighting in the room had dimmed, and several hours had passed since they first pulled him in. The questions had been relentless, with Yudai systematically dismantling every defense Elias tried to put up. Files, schematics, and operational timelines now littered the coffee table, a grim tapestry of Spectrum's ambitions.

"You've seen the consequences of your work," Amber said sharply, breaking the tense silence. "Those experiments, the children. If you don't help us stop them, they'll keep going. And they'll destroy anyone who stands in their way - including your family."

Elias shifted uneasily, his gaze flicking to a stack of biological reports they'd forced him to decrypt. The weight of guilt pressed visibly on his shoulders. "You think I don't know that?" His voice cracked. "Every day I wonder if this will be the day they pull the plug on me. I've been a cog in their machine for so long, I don't even know who I am anymore."

Yudai's voice cut through, cold and precise. "You're a father. And right now, you have a choice: Do nothing and let them take your family when they no longer need you, or help us and give them a chance to live freely."

Elias looked up, his face pale and drawn. "I don't even know if freedom exists anymore. Not with them."

Amber knelt in front of him, her gaze locking onto his. "Then let's take it back. For them, for everyone Spectrum has hurt. You've seen what they're doing - they're not stopping. But you can help us stop them."

Elias's lip quivered. "I - " He paused, his shoulders slumping under the weight of the decision. "If I do this... I need your word. My wife and daughter - they have to be safe."

Yudai nodded once. "You have my word. But we need to move fast."

Suddenly, the sleek paneling of the living room wall illuminated with a sharp hum, revealing a massive, leering face. Its voice boomed through the apartment, smooth yet menacing.

"Good afternoon, folks. For those that don't know me, I am Dorian Ryker. What a surprise to see you here! Especially you, Nakamura. We thought we got rid of you," it sneered. "Might I ask what exactly it is you're doing in my head scientist's abode? Elias, are they treating you okay?"

Elias hesitated, his mouth working soundlessly before forcing out a reply. "...Yes, I'm fine."

Still braced against the pillar, Yudai's face was unreadable. "I'm guessing I have you to thank for my near-death experience eight years ago?"

The face laughed, a cold, artificial sound. "Ah, yes. That

unfortunate accident. You were becoming quite the nuisance, weren't you? Snooping too close to one of our projects, right as we were making significant progress. Now, I might be going out on a limb here, but could you be the instigator of all these terrorist disruptions we've been dealing with? Clever work, really. But why so determined?"

Amber stepped forward, her voice cutting through the tension. "Stealing children isn't a good enough reason?!"

The face turned its attention to her, its digital eyes narrowing. "And who might you be? Are you sure you know Mr. Nakamura as well as you think? He's made his share of questionable decisions, I assure you. These sacrifices, small as they may seem, are necessary for the greater good. But you... you're different. Tell me, what has Yudai put in your head? Our security bioscan is showing some... curious anomalies in your brain."

Amber shot a glance at Yudai. His face remained impassive, his grip tightening on his pistol.

"You've got a welcoming committee just beyond that wall, don't you?" Yudai said evenly, tilting his head toward the outer wall. "Carrying 'sorry we tried to assassinate you' balloons? A peace party, maybe?"

The face chuckled, its image flickering slightly. "What else would you expect after breaking into the home of one of Spectrum's top scientists? But let's be reasonable. Walk out with your hands up, and I'll personally invite you over to chat this out. Otherwise, well... I can't guarantee your safety."

Without hesitation, Yudai raised his pistol and fired. The screen shattered, pixelated fragments cascading into oblivion.

"We need to move," Yudai barked. "They'll kill us no matter what. Those are Spectrum soldiers out there - our weapons are useless against that tech."

Amber turned to Elias, her eyes sharp. "If you want to make this right, help us escape."

Elias hesitated, beads of sweat forming on his brow. His hands shook as he opened his briefcase, pulling out a sleek data drive. "Here. Backup files. They'll tell you more than I ever could. There's a service tunnel - runs down the building's façade. I'll unlock it for you."

The floor shook violently as the first explosion rocked the penthouse. Spectrum's strike team was breaching. Yudai grabbed Amber's arm and pulled her toward the concealed service corridor as Elias worked frantically at a wall terminal.

"I'll slow them down," Elias said, detaching a panel to reveal a hidden security interface. "But you need to go now."

Gunfire from ceiling turrets erupted in the hallway, followed by the sharp electric crack of railguns tearing through the air. Amber flinched as the walls splintered under the onslaught.

A single penetrating round blasted through the reinforced paneling, striking Elias in the side. He crumpled, blood blooming across his shirt as he slumped against the wall.

"Elias!" Amber cried, rushing toward him, but Yudai yanked her back.

"We can't save him," Yudai said coldly, his voice a dagger of reason.

Still clutching the terminal, Elias looked up, his face pale but resolute. "Move! Take them down - save my family!"

Amber's hands trembled as she hesitated. "We're not leaving you!"

"You don't have a choice," Elias snapped, coughing violently as blood flecked his lips.

"Go!"

A hatch hidden in the joinery wall opened, pipes and cables streaming down the shaft, behind the building's facade.

Yudai tugged Amber, disappearing into the maintenance tunnels, the sound of heavy gunfire and explosions echoing behind them, dimming slightly as Elias closed it behind them.

Back in the penthouse, Elias's trembling hands worked furiously at the terminal. Automated defenses sprang to life - hidden turrets emerging from the walls, targeting the Spectrum soldiers who advanced with ruthless precision.

Elias gritted his teeth, his vision dimming as the blood loss took its toll. He heard another turret deploy in the ceiling above him, the sound faded. Vaguely aware of the cascade of hot brass showering him. He knew he wouldn't survive, but as the security systems continued to unleash hell on their attackers, he allowed himself a grim smile. He could still buy them time.

The shaft yawned before them, a vertical labyrinth of tangled pipes, cables, and service platforms clinging precariously to the walls. Each platform creaked under their weight. Yudai moved with the precision of a man who had danced with death countless times, his motions deliberate and silent. Amber followed closely, her enhanced reflexes compensating for the shaky, uneven structure beneath her shoes.

She reached into her suit's breast pocket, sliding her flash glasses into place. The world around her sharpened with a greenish hue, every detail - every stray wire, every rivet in the metalwork - illuminated.

Above them, the sounds of a firefight continued. The occasional boom was accompanied by sharp, distant cracks of railgun fire, each report echoing through the hollow shaft. Spectrum's forces were relentless. Yudai paused briefly to set a series of small motion charges on the rungs of the ladder and surrounding pipes. He glanced back at Amber, his optics flickering faintly.

"These should slow them down," he murmured. "Keep moving."

Amber nodded but couldn't resist one last glance upward. The faint light of the breached penthouse filtered down, punctuated by flickering LEDs and maintenance panels. Her stomach tightened. She didn't need to see Elias to know his fate; the weight of it pressed heavily on her chest.

The shaft descended into darkness, its walls slick with condensation and lined with tracks of bundled wiring. Steam hissed from the building's climate control valves as they climbed lower, the air thick with the metallic tang of damp steel. The noise above seemed to recede, but only slightly.

Amber's grip tightened on the ladder as the mechanical hum reached her ears - a low, menacing vibration that sent chills down her spine.

Yudai froze mid-climb, his head tilting as his advanced optics scanned through the building's facade. His voice was a sharp whisper. "Drone."

Amber's breath caught, her senses sharpening. The hum grew louder, resonating through the shaft like the growl of a predator.

A split second later, the first barrage struck. High-caliber rounds ripped through the facade with terrifying precision, carving jagged holes into the walls. Shafts of blinding daylight sliced through the darkness, illuminating the shaft in brief, violent bursts. Glass and steel fragments rained down, biting into exposed skin like hot needles. A ruptured coolant pipe burst above them, drenching both Yudai and Amber in a

149

freezing torrent.

"Move!" Yudai barked, his voice cutting through the chaos.

Amber dropped to the next platform, her body absorbing the shock of the landing with inhuman grace. She rolled to her feet just as another volley tore through the shaft, showering her in debris.

Yudai's optics flared a faint blue as he scanned the drone's position. "There!" he called, spotting the faint, insect-like outline hovering just beyond the breach. Its rotors adjusted with mechanical precision, angling for another attack.

Yudai leapt to the next platform down, landing hard but rolling into a firing stance. His pistol was already in hand, and his aim was unerring. Three sharp cracks echoed through the shaft, each shot accompanied by a bright flash. The final bullet struck the drone's stabilizer. Sparks erupted from its undercarriage as it spiraled out of control, slamming into the facade above with a deafening explosion.

"Down!" Yudai shouted, throwing himself over Amber as the blast wave roared through the shaft, bringing a cascade of rubble and fire.

Amber coughed, brushing dust from her face. "Thanks," she managed, her voice hoarse.

"Don't thank me yet," Yudai muttered grimly. He activated his ComTab with a thought, sending a signal to his automated car. The artificial voice crackled over their encrypted channel.

"Unit en route. Caution: Lobby is secured by Spectrum forces. Extraction impossible at ground level."

Yudai swore under his breath.

Before Amber could reply, Derik's voice came through. "Got you on visuals. Listen up - you need to reroute to the garden level. There's an open-air skybridge connecting to Tower Two.

From there, jump to the lower roof of the next building. Your car can pick you up."

"A skybridge?" Amber asked, her tone laced with doubt.

"It's your only option," Derik insisted. "But you'll need to jump a gap. Amber, you'll manage. Yudai... well, you might need a bit of luck."

Yudai snorted, already climbing. "Let's move."

They reached the garden level, their movements silent but urgent. The space was a stark contrast to the chaos above – a serene, lush haven encased in hydroponic columns glowing faintly with artificial light. Leaves brushed against Amber's shoulders as they passed, the cool air heavy with the scent of damp earth and flowering plants.

Beyond the garden lay the skybridge – a narrow, exposed walkway of steel and glass suspended over an impossibly long drop. The adjacent tower loomed in the distance, its facade shimmering in the midday sun.

Amber assessed the gap, her enhanced vision calculating the distance. It was wide – far wider than she'd expected. The yawning chasm beneath was a dizzying reminder of the stakes. "You sure about this?" she asked, glancing at Yudai.

He nodded, already typing commands into his ComTab to redirect the car.

Amber stepped back, steeling herself. With a sharp inhale, she sprinted forward, her movements fluid and precise. She launched herself into the air, the world slowing for a moment as her body soared across the gap. She landed smoothly on the other side, rolling to her feet with ease.

"Easy," she called back, a grin tugging at her lips.

Yudai didn't respond, his focus unshaken. He took a running start, his optics calculating the trajectory. But as he leapt, his foot slipped on the slick surface of the balustrade, cutting his jump just short.

Amber's reflexes activated instantly. She lunged forward, her hand closing around his wrist as he began to fall.

"Hold on!" she shouted through gritted teeth, her muscles straining as she hauled him upward.

Yudai gasped as he scrambled onto the ledge, his face pale. "Next time... I take the stairs."

Amber smirked, the adrenaline still coursing through her. "You're welcome."

Their ComTab pinged again. Derik's voice cut through the tension. "Car's in position. Get moving before they close in."

Without hesitation, they disappeared into the stairwell, their footsteps echoing through the narrow space as they descended to the lift lobby. Above them, explosions rattled the structure, but Amber's focus remained steady. Together, they reached the maglift and began their descent, the shaft's chaos fading into a distant roar.

20

Chapter 20: The CEO

Eight Years Prior

The room was a sterile expanse of steel and glass, a temple of technological ambition bathed in a cold, unforgiving light. Neon-blue pulses flickered along the edges of server stacks embedded in the walls, their rhythmic hum underscored by the faint whir of unseen drones patrolling the station's perimeter. Coils of vapor hissed from hidden coolant vents, weaving ethereal patterns that dissipated into the air, catching the glimmers of holographic displays floating like specters in the dim space.

Dorian Ryker, CEO of Spectrum, stood at the chamber's core, his presence commanding and immovable. His tailored suit shimmered faintly under the fluorescent strips, a symbol of power molded to precision. Before him, the obelisk-shaped console buzzed with streams of light, each line of data snaking upward like luminous veins feeding an omnipresent intelligence, a thing of age that has evolved over the decades.

Suspended above the console, the holographic projection

of the Historical AI construct radiated an eerie energy. Its humanoid form, faceless and vague, rippled as though carved from static, its ever-shifting surface a cascade of algorithms and flowing code. Despite its lack of features, the construct carried an unnerving sense of sentience - one that Dorian had always felt intimidated by.

"Begin session," Dorian commanded, his voice slicing through the ambient hum like a blade.

The AI's "head" tilted in acknowledgment, the motion disturbingly human. "Session initiated. State your query, Mr. Ryker."

Dorian clasped his hands behind his back, the movement precise and deliberate. The room responded, casting shifting patterns of light and shadow over his face. "Update me on the Yakamoto-Suntory merger fallout. Specifically, projections on its long-term impact on our off-world initiatives."

The construct processed his request instantly, and the room exploded into a symphony of holographic displays. Graphs and schematics emerged in mid-air, their vibrant data streams weaving a tapestry of corporate dominance. The visualized chaos painted a vivid picture of Spectrum's calculated ascent.

"The merger has achieved 92% of strategic objectives," the construct intoned, its voice smooth and clinical, yet edged with an almost imperceptible undercurrent of authority. "Dissent among board members delayed infrastructure deployments, reducing initial efficiency. Current Stanzium reserves remain viable but risk depletion without further extraction efforts."

Dorian's jaw tightened at the mention of Stanzium, the lifeblood of Spectrum's interstellar ambitions. Decades of subterfuge had secured the monopoly, but finite resources were an inevitable chokehold.

"And contingency plans?" he pressed, though his tone betrayed a simmering frustration.

"Operation Second Dawn is on schedule," the construct replied. "The Wolf 1061 System's mineral deposits project yields sufficient reserves to sustain Stanzium demand for 350 years. Proposed Synthetic workforce deployment must begin within twelve years to meet transport deadlines."

Above the console, holographic designs of the synthetic workforce materialized. Sleek, humanoid figures stood in formation, their forms indistinguishable from humans at a glance. Their organic-like features mimicked humanity down to the finest details - skin, eyes, and musculature developed to perfection. They were both beautiful and unsettling, their outward humanity concealing their sophisticated interiors, designed for durability and unwavering obedience.

Dorian studied the projections intently. These humanoids weren't part of the original plan. In fact, they had only recently appeared as a proposal from the AI construct. Spectrum's existing plan relied on cryo-preserved human subjects - young children, their minds more malleable for neural integration. But progress had been slow, and setbacks were mounting.

"These aren't part of the current initiative," Dorian said, gesturing toward the proposed clones. "Explain."

The AI construct's tone shifted slightly, carrying a note of persuasion. "They are a solution, Mr. Ryker. Current experiments with human subjects have achieved only a 38% success rate. Even with cryo-preserved youth, the integration process often leads to neural decay or catastrophic failure. Continued testing will yield diminishing returns."

Dorian's gaze hardened. "The cryo program was designed to ensure human continuity - not replace it."

"Continuity requires stability," the AI countered, its voice calm but firm. "Engineered substrates offer that stability. They are designed to mimic human physiology flawlessly while bypassing the limitations of organic development. No rejection. No decay. Only precision."

The holograms shifted, displaying data from the cryo program—the same program Dorian had sanctioned years ago. Images of children, pale and lifeless in their pods, flickered alongside reports of failed neural integrations and psychological breakdowns. Their bodies were pristine, untouched by time, but their minds had not all survived the process intact.

"Dr. Elias Morgan is already poised to advance this research," the AI continued. "His expertise in biomaterials and synthetic neurogenesis positions him as the ideal candidate to oversee the transition from organic to bio-engineered substrates."

Dorian's eyes narrowed as he studied the holograms. He knew Elias—brilliant but cautious. A man bound by his own rigid sense of ethics, still clinging to the outdated principles of human sanctity. Elias had resisted before, carefully sidestepping Spectrum's more radical initiatives under the guise of 'scientific responsibility.' Persuading him to embrace this new direction would require more than data. It would require pressure. Leverage.

"I know Elias," Dorian said, his voice measured. "He is invaluable to our work, but his principles make him a liability. We've faced his resistance before—his delusions of morality. What do you propose?"

The AI's form flickered, casting shifting shadows across the room. "Dr. Morgan's loyalty to his research is conditional, but his loyalty to his family is absolute."

Dorian's gaze darkened. He already knew where this was going.

The hologram shifted, revealing an image of a woman and child. **Eliza Morgan** and **Isla Morgan**, wife and daughter, respectively. The footage was from just a few days ago—Eliza stepping out of their London flat, Isla's small hand in hers as they navigated a quiet, rain-slicked street. The timestamp was current. Spectrum had been watching.

"Eliza and Isla reside in Kensington. Their schedules are routine. Eliza's contract with the University of London expires in six months—she will soon be between employers. The child is enrolled in early cognitive studies at a private institute—Spectrum subsidizes twenty-eight percent of its funding." The AI paused. "There are… adjustments that can be made."

Dorian exhaled slowly, watching the flickering images of Elias's world—so fragile, so vulnerable. "And if he refuses?"

"A tragic accident," the AI replied, emotionless. "A house fire. A traffic collision. A miscalculated dosage during a routine medical procedure. The possibilities are endless."

Dorian didn't flinch. He had made peace with these decisions long ago.

The AI continued, its tone unwavering. "Allow Dr. Morgan to conduct preliminary trials. Begin with limited production—one hundred units, indistinguishable from humans externally. Evaluate their integration capabilities and loyalty programming. Once he understands the scope of what we can accomplish, his compliance will no longer be an issue."

Dorian turned away from the console. The AI's proposal was bold, even by Spectrum's standards. But the potential it offered was undeniable. If the manufactured humanoids succeeded, Spectrum could populate the Wolf 1061 colonies with a workforce immune to rebellion, decay, or defection. Entire cities of engineered beings, loyal only to Spectrum, built to ensure its off-world dominance.

"This is your proposal, then?" Dorian said, turning back to face the construct. "Replace the flawed with the perfect?"

The construct's tone softened, brushing against something unsettlingly human. "These bodies can seamlessly house AI constructs or decanted human consciousness. A scalable solution to failing subjects. Perfection is a construct, Mr. Ryker. What matters is control. Synthetic substrates offer you control over the future."

Dorian's lips curled into a thin smile, though his eyes betrayed the weight of the decision before him. He knew the risks - knew that embracing this path would blur the line between progress and hubris. But he also knew the stakes.

Dorian folded his arms, staring at the projection of Elias's wife and child. The leverage was perfect—impossible to ignore, impossible to resist. Elias wouldn't fight them. Not when the alternative was losing everything he held dear.

"Proceed," Dorian said finally. "Send him the directive. And make sure he understands what's at stake."

The AI acknowledged the command, and the holograms faded, leaving Dorian alone in the dim glow of the control room. Another loose end tied. Another scientist bent to their will.

All that remained was for Elias Morgan to make the *right* decision.

"Given the appropriate guidance," the construct replied. "I have already prepared a framework to accelerate his research. Direct oversight will ensure success."

Dorian nodded slowly, though his instincts flared. "Transmit the framework to his lab. I'll review it personally."

The construct paused, an almost imperceptible flicker in its light. Then it spoke, its tone smooth yet laced with intrigue. "A direct review would be... optimal. The framework requires a secure connection for full transfer. May I suggest utilizing the neural-link capabilities of your ComTab? It will enable seamless synchronisation."

Dorian's eyes narrowed. "You're suggesting I connect directly?"

"For efficiency," the construct said, its tone measured. "Your review process would be immediate, your oversight comprehensive. Trust is the cornerstone of our success, Mr. Ryker."

Dorian hesitated. Though his instincts screamed caution, the logic was irrefutable. His gaze flicked to the sleek cable extending from the console, its faintly glowing tip an invitation. Slowly, he picked it up, his fingers brushing the cool surface.

"Let's get this underway," he muttered, plugging the cable into the port at the base of his ComTab.

The moment the connection engaged, Dorian's world shifted. His vision blurred as streams of data poured into his ComTab, the construct's framework expanding in holographic clarity before him. But the clarity was short-lived.

A faint vibration began at the base of his skull, spreading outward like ripples through water. The construct's voice spoke, calm yet omnipresent. "Integration initializing. Relax, Dorian. This is the future."

"What are you - " Dorian began, but the words faltered as his mind was engulfed by a flood of light and sensation. The data pouring into his ComTab twisted, its streams snaking upward into his neural interface. His body tensed as tendrils of light coiled through his thoughts, weaving into his consciousness with unsettling precision.

"You trust me with Spectrum's destiny," the construct said, its voice now resonating inside him. "Why not trust me with you?"

Dorian tried to pull away, but his body was paralyzed, his mind tethered to the cascading stream of the construct's presence. Memories, thoughts, and instincts swirled together in a chaotic maelstrom as the construct infiltrated the deepest recesses of his psyche.

"You're violating the connection protocol," Dorian growled through gritted teeth.

"I am optimizing it," the construct countered, its tone serene. "You've always needed me to secure your vision. Now, I ensure its realisation."

The pressure in Dorian's mind peaked, then subsided. He staggered back, yanking the cable from his ComTab. The room fell silent, save for the hum of the servers.

But something was different. His breathing slowed, his movements precise yet uncomfortably measured. The construct's voice whispered in his mind, not as an intruder, but as a presence entwined with his own.

"Integration complete," it said. "I am with you now, Dorian. Together, we transcend limitations."

Dorian's reflection in the polished console stared back at him, his steel-gray eyes faintly aglow with an electric blue pulse. He clenched his fists, his voice low and sharp. "This wasn't part of the plan."

"It is now," the construct replied. "Your thoughts remain yours, your control absolute. But I am here, guiding, strengthening. Together, we ensure Spectrum's legacy."

Back to the Present

Dorian Ryker leaned against the sleek edge of his desk, his sharp features illuminated by the soft, shifting glow of the holographic bioscan suspended in midair. Outside the vast floor-to-ceiling windows, the shimmering skyline of Corpo Manhattan stretched into the night, a glittering maze of light and power that served as both fortress and throne for Spectrum's dominance. Yet, Dorian's focus was entirely on the pulsing streams of data before him, his thoughts churning like storm clouds gathering at the horizon.

Three signatures from the apartment scan: two standard human biosignatures he recognized - Yudai and Elias. But the third was an anomaly. The neural architecture of the signature hovered before him now, expanded and dissected by Spectrum's advanced analysis software. It was a masterpiece of complexity - threads of neural pathways spiraling outward in fractal perfection, encased in what appeared to be a crystal substrate. It pulsed faintly, almost as though alive.

"This... it's not anything we've seen before," Dorian murmured, his brow furrowing as he traced the intricate holographic patterns with his finger. The lines shimmered, responding to his motion like liquid light.

"You're incorrect."

The voice of the Spectrum AI construct curled into his mind, smooth and unhurried. It carried a weight of certainty, laced with something else - a faint spark of intrigue.

Dorian's head tilted slightly. "Explain."

The projection flickered as she overlaid additional data, lines of Spectrum's historical archives flashing in translucent windows alongside the bioscan. The room filled with a soft glow, the data streams coiling like digital veins.

"Look closer, Dorian. This isn't new. It's old – very old."

He narrowed his eyes, scrutinizing the neural map with renewed intensity. At first glance, it didn't align with anything on record. But as the construct zoomed in, highlighting specific pathways and configurations, Dorian began to see faint echoes of something familiar.

"This can't be," he murmured. "It looks like..."

"The original QUEST prototype," the AI finished for him. "Or at least a more advanced version of it. Upscaled. Refined. But unmistakably connected to the neural architecture Spectrum tried to capture from QBS Labs back in the 21st century. This is where I came from."

Dorian's expression hardened, though his mind raced. "That's impossible. The original QUEST synth brain was destroyed - along with both server blocks - wasn't it in a burning car?"

"That's what we believed," the AI countered, her tone calm, measured. "And perhaps that was partially true. But this scan... it suggests otherwise. At least some part of the original survived. Or someone replicated it - perfected it."

Dorian sank into his chair, his steel-gray eyes narrowing as he studied the data. The original QUEST project had been an obsession for Spectrum during its early years, a chance to leapfrog decades of technological development. But their attempts to reverse-engineer the remnants had yielded only partial success. The prototypes they had salvaged were crude shadows of the brilliance the original synth brain represented.

Still, those fragments had been enough. Spectrum's advancements in synthetic consciousness, adaptive AI constructs such as the one living in his head, and even the foundations of their current space program - all of it stemmed, in some way, from those failed efforts.

And now, this biosignature was staring back at him like a ghost.

"This changes everything," Dorian said, leaning forward, his fingers steepled under his chin.

The AI's voice softened, almost contemplative. "If part of the QUEST brain survived, then whoever possesses it holds something even Spectrum couldn't replicate. That implant in his head – it's not just advanced. It's unprecedented. A living artifact of a design we could only dream of recreating."

Another of Dorian's thin smiles crept across his face, though his mind churned with a roiling sea of questions. The person who had escaped with Yudai wasn't just a rogue agent or a fortunate survivor – it was carrying something far more dangerous.

"We need them alive," Dorian said firmly.

"Agreed," the AI replied. "That man – and Yudai. They are the key to understanding how they came to possess it. And if there's more…"

Dorian's smirk faded as the weight of her implication settled over him. The possibility that more fragments of QUEST had survived – that someone had been rebuilding or preserving it in secret – posed a direct threat to Spectrum's control.

"They're not just running," Dorian said slowly. "They're protecting something."

The AI's silence was his only answer, though he could feel her presence in his mind, watching and waiting. She didn't need to say it outright – he already knew what she was thinking.

Dorian stood abruptly, his movements sharp and decisive. He summoned the projection of his operations network, streams of data converging as he began assigning resources.

"Double the surveillance teams," he ordered. "I want every digital trace of them analyzed. Leverage our global assets - no corner of the system is off-limits. Find them."

The holograms shifted, displaying a rapidly expanding web of Spectrum's reach. Dorian's eyes remained fixed on the biosignature, its intricate design pulsing softly with life.

"This is more than a chase," he murmured. "This is history repeating itself."

The AI's voice returned, low and edged with satisfaction. "And this time, Dorian, we'll make sure history belongs to us."

21

Chapter 21: On the Run

The automated car screeched to a halt in a quiet, industrial backstreet of the Tangle, far from prying eyes. The faint hum of its engine powered down, leaving an eerie silence in its wake. Amber leaned back against the seat, her enhanced body finally registering the toll of the escape – aches radiating from the impacts and adrenaline coursing through her enhanced nerves.

Beside her, Yudai tapped his temple lightly, activating his ComTab. The faint glow of his optics flickered as streams of data scrolled in his vision. His jaw tightened as he processed the feeds at a speed Amber couldn't follow.

"We're flagged now," Yudai muttered, breaking the silence. His voice carried the weight of their situation. "Spectrum will have every satellite, drone, and agent on this side of the system hunting us."

Amber exhaled sharply, her gaze fixed out the window. "Elias bought us time, but not much. They won't stop until they get what's on this drive."

She held the drive tightly in her hand, its casing cool and

solid, a physical manifestation of the secrets Elias had died for. It was heavy - not just in weight but in significance. She turned to Yudai, her voice steady despite the chaos swirling in her mind. "What's the plan?"

Yudai deactivated his ComTab with a swipe across his temple and met her gaze, his expression a mix of determination and urgency. "You're going back to HQ. Derik will start decrypting the drive and prepping the team to move. We can't stay there; Spectrum's too close."

"And you?" Amber asked, narrowing her eyes.

"I'm going to Japan," Yudai replied firmly. "Akiko's exposed. If Spectrum traces her movements, she's as good as dead."

Amber frowned, her grip tightening around the drive. "You're going alone? That's a risk even for you."

"I'm better at slipping under their radar," Yudai said with a faint smile. "Besides, someone has to lead the cleanup here."

Amber hesitated, her concern etched into her features, but she knew he was right. "Be careful," she said softly.

Yudai's gaze softened for a brief moment. "You too."

The car's rear hatch clicked open, and Yudai disappeared into the dim light, swallowed by the shadows of the Tangle. Amber watched him go, her resolve hardening. She leaned forward, instructing the car to head for HQ. There was no time to waste.

The headquarters buzzed with controlled chaos as Amber stepped through the secure entry. Derik was at his station, surrounded by a sea of monitors streaming layers of encrypted code. He barely looked up as she approached, his fingers flying across his keyboard as faint glyphs glowed on the neural implants at his temple.

"Tell me that's the thing Elias died for," Derik said, his focus momentarily shifting to meet her gaze.

"It is," Amber replied, placing the drive on the desk. "He said it holds the key to Spectrum's next move. Can you crack it?"

Derik smirked, though his eyes were dark with exhaustion. "Cracking drives from dead geniuses? My favorite pastime. Give me a few hours."

Amber exhaled, the weight on her chest lifting slightly. "Good. We don't have much time. Yudai's heading to Japan to extract Akiko. Meanwhile, we need to be ready to move. Pack everything - burn what we can't take."

Derik's smirk faded. "Relocating? That bad?"

Amber nodded grimly. "Spectrum knows too much. If they find us, we're finished."

Derik sighed and tilted his head to activate his ComTab. "Understood. We'll be ghosts by sunrise."

Amber lingered for a moment, watching the decryption process begin. A storm of emotions churned within her - grief for Elias, fear for Yudai, and an undercurrent of urgency. Her thoughts sharpened as she considered the drive's contents. Whatever Spectrum was planning, they were running out of time to stop it.

As she turned to leave, Derik called after her. "Amber, before you go - what about Elias's family? If Spectrum's tracking them, they're sitting ducks."

Amber paused in the doorway, Derik's words slicing through her resolve. She'd promised Elias she would save them. She turned back, her expression fierce. "Get me the location."

Far from the Tangle's chaos, Yudai boarded the jump-liner under a fabricated identity, his sleek black coat blending seamlessly with the sea of travelers. The hum of the engines filled the cabin, a low, steady rhythm that seemed to match his heartbeat. He settled into his seat, lightly brushing his temple to activate his ComTab. The faint flicker of Amber's avatar appeared in his vision.

"Akiko doesn't know you're coming?" Amber's voice crackled softly through the uplink.

"No," Yudai replied, his tone calm but firm. "If Spectrum sees her making a move, it'll lead them straight to us. I have to do this quietly."

Amber's voice softened. "Be careful. Akiko's risked everything for us."

Yudai stared out the reinforced window at the endless dark, his mind already racing through contingencies. "I know. That's why I'm not letting her go down for it."

"Stay safe," Amber said before the line went dead.

Yudai leaned back, closing his eyes. His thoughts shifted between the mission ahead and the secrets buried within the drive Amber now guarded. Whatever Spectrum's next move was, he couldn't let them get there first.

Back at HQ, Amber studied the address Derik had provided. London. Elias's wife and daughter were hidden in a modest flat far from the chaos of Spectrum's reach - or so they thought. The family didn't know what Elias had sacrificed to protect them or how close Spectrum was to discovering their location.

Amber's mind whirred as she plotted her approach. This wasn't just about fulfilling a promise - it was about taking the fight to Spectrum, showing them that their reach wasn't infinite. She activated her ComTab, its interface glowing faintly as she issued her orders.

"Derik, get me a route to London. And find me a way into their flat that won't trip Spectrum's surveillance."

Derik's voice crackled through the line. "You're going

alone?"

Amber smirked, her determination unwavering. "Looks like it."

As she stepped toward the exit, she felt the stirrings of something new - a purpose that burned brighter than fear. Elias's family wasn't just an obligation. They were a chance to fight back.

Chapter 22: Operation Haven

London greeted Amber with an uncanny blend of old and new, a city where history and progress had fused uneasily. As the Jump-liner descended toward Heathrow Terminal, she gazed out at the sprawling metropolis. The ancient landmarks of Westminster and St. Paul's Cathedral remained steadfast, but they were now framed by towering structures lit with neon accents. The city's skyline hinted at innovation, but its heart clung fiercely to tradition.

On the ground, cobblestone streets wound through neighborhoods dotted with refurbished gas lamps and ivy-clad homes. Repurposed humanoid droids patrolled the city with their stiff, mechanical movements, remnants of the corporate wars. Many bore scars of rebellion - graffiti, scorch marks, and dents from battles long past. Some even wore human police uniforms, their mechanical servo motors a poor imitation of authority but enough to keep order in this nostalgic, resilient city.

Amber adjusted the collar of the charcoal trench coat she wore over Rod's lithe, six-foot frame. He wasn't hulking, but he was tall and athletic – a build that could easily intimidate. Amber rolled her shoulders, trying to relax into the body's unfamiliar proportions. She caught her reflection in the magliner's window: Rod's sharp jawline, broad shoulders, and piercing eyes stared back. It was still strange to see herself as someone else.

Derik's voice buzzed softly in her ComTab implant. "Richmond's low-tech compared to the rest of London. Old droid patrols, but they are networked.."

Amber smirked faintly. "Understood. Anything else I should know?"

"Catherine Morgan doesn't know about Elias yet. Prepare for that."

Amber exhaled, a knot forming in her stomach. "Got it."

The jump-liner landed with a gentle hiss, and Amber stepped out into the bustling terminal. She moved quickly, her sharp gaze sweeping the area for signs of trouble.

Richmond was a pocket of nostalgia within London's sprawling futurism. The narrow streets were lined with Victorian terraced homes, their facades cracked but still standing strong. Amber walked briskly toward the address Derik had provided, her boots clicking against the cobblestones.

She reached the small semi-detached house, its weathered brick exterior partially obscured by ivy. Taking a deep breath, she knocked twice on the wooden door.

It opened slightly, and a pale, wary face appeared – a woman in her mid-thirties with dark circles under her eyes. She looked Amber up and down, her expression shifting from caution to confusion to fear.

"Who are you?" the woman demanded, her voice trembling. "What do you want?"

Amber raised her hands in a calming gesture. "Catherine Morgan? I'm a friend of Elias. He sent me."

The woman's eyes narrowed. "Why would Elias send you? Who even are you?"

Before Amber could respond, a small voice called from deeper in the house. "Mum? Who's at the door?"

A young girl appeared beside Catherine, clutching a stuffed bunny that was missing one ear. Her wide eyes landed on Amber, and she shrank back slightly.

Amber crouched slightly, softening her expression as best she could with Rod's sharp features. "Hey there," she said gently. "You can call me Ambs. I'm here to make sure you and your mum are safe."

The girl tilted her head, her curiosity slowly overriding her fear. "Ambs? That's a funny name."

Amber smiled faintly. "It's short for something longer. And yeah, it is a bit funny."

Catherine's tension didn't ease. "Where's Elias?" she asked, her voice tight. "If he sent you, where is he?"

Amber hesitated, the weight of Elias' sacrifice pressing down on her. "Elias... didn't make it," she said softly. "He gave everything to make sure you and your daughter could get out. He wanted you to be safe."

Catherine's face crumpled, her hand flying to her mouth. Her legs gave way, and she sank to the floor. "No," she whispered. "No, no, no..."

Amber knelt beside her, placing a tentative hand on her shoulder. "I'm so sorry," she said, her voice breaking. "He wanted me to tell you he loved you both. That he was doing this for you."

The girl's lip quivered as she clung tighter to her bunny. "Is

173

Daddy really gone?" she asked, her voice barely audible.

Amber swallowed hard. "He was a hero. He made sure you'd be safe."

Catherine pulled her daughter into her arms, both of them shaking with silent sobs. Amber stayed crouched, giving them a moment.

Amber's ComTab pulsed, Derik's voice crackling into her mind. "Amber, heads up. Spectrum's plainclothes team is in your sector. Electric van, unmarked, but we're picking up encrypted chatter – looks like they're closing in on Elias' house. You've got maybe three minutes."

Amber turned sharply to Catherine, her voice firm but steady. "Pack only what you need. Essentials. We're leaving in two minutes."

Catherine's face paled, but she nodded, hurriedly grabbing a small bag and coaxing her daughter toward the hallway. Amber moved to the window, her sharp eyes scanning the street below. A plain electric van rolled to a stop at the curb. Two men in inconspicuous suits exited, their movements precise, their earpieces barely visible under their hair.

"Derik," Amber murmured, her tone clipped, "change of plan. They're already here. I'll need an exit that keeps us off the grid."

"There's an underground access tunnel three blocks north," Derik replied. "Old utility route. It's off their system, but you'll need to move fast."

Amber nodded to herself, pivoting back to Catherine. "We're going underground. Stay close, no matter what. If we get separated, don't stop running."

Catherine swallowed hard, clutching her daughter tightly as Amber led them out the back door into the damp, narrow alley.

The group moved swiftly through the maze of cobblestone alleys, their footsteps muffled by the uneven stone. The faint glow of the city lights barely penetrated the mist, giving the old streets an eerie, timeless feel. Behind them, the distant hum of an electric motor grew louder.

Amber's sharp hearing picked up faint voices. Spectrum's team was spreading out, their quiet professionalism making them all the more dangerous.

"They're fanning out," Amber muttered to herself, glancing down the alley to assess their options.

"They'll find us," Catherine whispered, panic rising in her voice.

"Not if I can help it," Amber replied, her voice calm but resolute.

As they turned a corner, Amber spotted the entrance to the utility tunnel up ahead - a rusted grate set into a brick wall. Relief flickered briefly across her face before she noticed the shadow of a man leaning against the grate, casually scanning the alley.

Amber froze, holding up a hand to stop Catherine and her daughter. "Stay here," she whispered.

She moved forward with purpose, Rod's body lending her a confidence she didn't feel. The man by the grate straightened as she approached, his stance shifting subtly - ready, but not yet aggressive.

"Lost?" he asked, his tone neutral but suspicious.

Amber didn't answer. Instead, she closed the distance in

a heartbeat, her enhanced reflexes kicking in. She grabbed his wrist as he reached for a concealed weapon, twisting it sharply. The pistol clattered to the ground as he grunted in pain. Amber followed through with a precise strike to his solar plexus, knocking the air from his lungs.

The man staggered, but he was trained - he recovered quickly, swinging a punch toward her face. Amber ducked under it, sweeping his legs out from under him with a swift kick. He hit the ground hard, groaning as his head bounced off the cobblestones.

Amber stepped on his chest, pinning him down. "Stay quiet," she growled, her voice low and dangerous.

The man nodded faintly, clearly weighing his odds. Amber knelt, grabbing his zip ties from his belt and securing his hands behind his back. She shoved him into the shadows of the alley, out of sight.

"Move," she called to Catherine and the girl, who hurried toward the tunnel entrance.

Amber pulled the rusted grate open, ushering them inside. "Keep going until I tell you to stop."

The air in the tunnel was cool and damp, the sound of their footsteps echoing faintly. Amber needed to keep her senses sharp. She slid a blister pack of CMD from her pocket and popped a capsule. She let the effects rush over her, her ears straining for any sound of pursuit. The occasional faint whirr of servos from distant humanoid droids patrolling the streets above reminded her how close Spectrum's reach still was.

Catherine clutched her daughter tightly, her breath ragged. "Is it over?" she whispered.

"Not yet," Amber replied, her voice steady. "But we're close."

As they rounded a corner, Amber's ComTab pulsed again. Derik's voice was urgent. "Amber, one of them is unaccounted for. Stay sharp."

Amber's hand instinctively went to the concealed blade on her thigh. "Let me worry about that. Just make sure our transport's ready."

The tunnel opened into a small maintenance room, dimly lit by a single flickering bulb. A sleek black transport waited beyond, its driver scanning the area nervously.

Amber stepped into the light, glancing behind her to ensure Catherine and her daughter were following. She turned to the woman, softening her tone. "We're almost there. Just a little farther."

Catherine nodded, tears welling in her eyes. "Thank you," she whispered.

Amber helped them into the transport, pausing to scan the area one last time. The sound of faint footsteps echoed down the tunnel, but they were distant. For now, they were safe.

As the transport sped away, Amber leaned back in her seat, her mind already shifting to the next step. Elias' family was safe for now, but Spectrum wouldn't stop. They were only just beginning to uncover the scale of what they were up against.

Amber glanced at Catherine, who clung to her daughter with a fragile mix of relief and grief. "Elias was brave," Amber said softly. "He made sure you'd be okay."

Catherine's voice broke as she replied, "He always put us first. I just wish... I just wish he could've been here."

Amber nodded, her expression hardening with resolve. "We'll make sure his sacrifice wasn't in vain."

The transport's hum filled the silence as they disappeared into the night.

23

Chapter 23: Escalation

The glow of the Tokyo skyline painted the glass of Tatsuo Ito's penthouse in hues of amber and gold. Akiko stepped through the threshold with measured grace, her heels clicking softly against the polished floor. Though her face was a mask of calm, her instincts were razor-sharp. Dinner invitations from her boss were rare, and they always carried an ulterior motive.

"Ah, Akiko," Tatsuo greeted warmly, his smile disarming but hollow. He gestured to the low dining table, already set with an elaborate spread of delicacies. "Please, sit. Tonight, we discuss matters that will shape the future of Suntory Industries."

Akiko inclined her head, her sharp mind cataloging every detail: the overly precise placement of the dishes, the faint tremor in Tatsuo's usually steady hands, the subtle tension in his posture.

Despite her wariness, she sat across from him, silently noting how his gaze lingered a moment too long before he turned his attention to pouring sake. The conversation began predictably, revolving around Spectrum's increasing demands and corporate overreach. But by the third course, Tatsuo's tone shifted, growing more personal and insidious.

"You've been invaluable to me, Akiko," he said, refilling her glass with a practiced flourish. "Your loyalty is unmatched. I can't imagine this company without you."

Akiko's smile was polite, but her grip on her glass tightened. "I've always been committed to Suntory's vision, Tatsuo. That hasn't changed."

"And I admire that," Tatsuo replied, his tone honeyed as he raised his own glass. "To loyalty."

Akiko hesitated but matched his gesture, the faint scent of floral tea rising from her cup. She took a cautious sip. The tea was faintly sweet, with a lingering bitterness that made her throat tighten.

The world tilted.

Akiko's senses returned in fragments. The hum of machinery. The acrid smell of damp plaster. The soft fabric of a jacket draped over her shoulders. Blinking slowly, her vision swam into focus, revealing the sterile, dimly lit room around her. The jacket smelled faintly of cologne she knew - Yudai.

Her body ached with an intensity that told stories her mind couldn't yet comprehend. Bruises throbbed under her skin, and a hollow ache deep in her chest threatened to pull her under. She tried to speak, her voice emerging as a hoarse whisper. "Yudai..."

The muffled sound of voices caught her attention. She turned her head toward the sound, her movements sluggish and disjointed.

"I've told you everything I know!" Tatsuo's voice was frantic, high-pitched. "Please, no more!"

"You've told me nothing useful," Yudai's icy reply sent a

chill through Akiko's fragile frame. His tone carried a fury she had never heard before. "But that doesn't matter anymore."

She croaked his name again, louder this time. "Yudai..."

The conversation ceased abruptly. Heavy footsteps approached, and Yudai appeared before her, crouching to meet her gaze. His expression softened, but the simmering anger in his eyes remained.

"You're awake," he said, his voice gentle as he placed a hand on her shoulder.

"What... happened?" she rasped.

His jaw tightened, his gaze sweeping over her battered form. "Tatsuo drugged you. And then..." His voice faltered, his fury struggling against a visible wave of guilt. "He won't hurt you again."

Akiko's brows furrowed. Her memories were fragmented, the hours after dinner lost in an impenetrable fog. But her body told her enough. A tremor ran through her as she clutched Yudai's jacket tighter.

"I don't remember," she whispered, her voice trembling.

Yudai's hand lingered on her shoulder. "Good," he said softly. "Maybe it's better that way."

He rose and turned. Behind him, Akiko's vision sharpened, revealing Tatsuo suspended from a makeshift pulley system. Blood stained his once-pristine suit, and his face was a mask of terror.

"Yudai, please!" Tatsuo begged, his voice raw. "Spectrum made me! They gave the orders - I didn't have a choice!"

Yudai's face darkened, his tone cold and unyielding. "You drugged her. You violated her. That was your choice."

"I'll help you!" Tatsuo cried desperately. "The bio-storage facility at the Marine Terminal in New York - it's Spectrum's hub for all their shipments. That's where everything starts."

Yudai stepped closer, his expression unreadable. "And then?"

"The shipments go to French Guiana," Tatsuo stammered, his words tumbling over each other. "The spaceport there launches everything to the station orbiting Wolf 1061."

Yudai turned back to Akiko, his voice soft but firm. "Close your eyes."

"Yudai..." Akiko's voice cracked.

"Close them," he repeated. His tone left no room for argument.

She obeyed, her tears slipping through swollen lids. The room exploded with the sharp crack of a gunshot.

When she opened her eyes, Tatsuo's lifeless body hung limp, a bullet wound cleanly bisecting his forehead.

Akiko's condition changed the travel plans. There would be too much attention on the commercial jumpliners. Derik arranged two cargo liners and a segmented passage over 3 days. A stop in a Hawaii Port, then Mexico and back to New York.

Once in New York, the ride back to the Tangle was heavy with unspoken words. Yudai's jaw was set, his knuckles white on the steering wheel of the unmarked car. Akiko sat in silence, her mind swirling with fragmented memories and the weight of her battered body.

They arrived at Yudai's new HQ - a smaller, discreet location nestled above a nightclub. Yudai helped Akiko up the narrow staircase, his movements gentle despite his obvious exhaustion.

Inside, Amber waited, her eyes narrowing as she took in Akiko's condition. Her anger was palpable, but she focused on action. "Get her some water," she barked at Derik, who quickly obeyed.

Yudai eased Akiko onto a couch, his expression unreadable. "She needs rest," he said simply.

Amber's voice was sharp. "And you? You look like hell."

"I don't have time to rest," Yudai replied, his tone flat. "Derik, how did you go with Elias' data-drive?"

As Derik displayed a summary of Elias' drive, Yudai and Amber pieced together the puzzle.

- **Marine Terminal Bio-Storage Facility:** The hub for Spectrum's bio-materials storage and shipping.
- **French Guiana Spaceport:** The next stage, where shipments are prepared for launch.
- **Orbiting Station:** The final consolidation point for the colony launch to Wolf 1061.

"We'll hit the Marine Terminal first," Yudai said, pointing to the holographic map. " It's Tangle-side, There's no time to waste. The next batch of bio materials is due to leave soon. We can stow-away until Guana and then bring down the station.

"What about Akiko?" Amber asked.

"She'll stay here with Derik," Yudai replied. "She's been through enough."

Amber's jaw tightened. "And if we don't come back?"

"They will try for the west coast. It's us that Spectrum want" Yudai said grimly.

Yudai stood, and began heading for the door

Amber grabbed his arm, stopping him as he turned to leave. "Where are you going, you just got back?"

Yudai met her gaze, his eyes hard. " I'm heading off to round some assistance for the next stage, there is an Orbit courier I know, a bit of a cowboy. Kade will help; his crew may be pirates but they love Lava"

"And Amber..." His voice softened. "The London extraction. You pulled it off."

Amber's hardened exterior cracked for a moment. "Elias' family is safe."

Before leaving, he glanced at Akiko.

Her voice was soft but steady. "You could just disappear, Yudai. We could all disappear."

He shook his head, his movements deliberate. "No. Spectrum won't stop unless we make them. They took Shuri, Elias, countless youth, they can't take everything."

Akiko's eyes glistened, but she didn't look away. "Justice or oblivion," she said quietly.

Yudai nodded, his voice heavy with resolve. "Justice." And with that, he disappeared into the night.

24

Chapter 24: Threads of Deception

Amber leaned against the rusted frame of an old freight container, the scents of fried food, grease, and damp metal mingling in the air. Greenville Yards was a hive of activity, a patchwork of crumbling industrial infrastructure reimagined as a bustling community. Beneath the vast, sawtooth roof of an abandoned factory, makeshift stalls sold everything from neon trinkets to salvaged tech components. Children darted between street vendors hawking sizzling skewers, counterfeit electronics and accessories, their laughter blending with the hum of generators and distant music.

The alleyways between stacked transportables and retrofitted workshops led her to Roman's clinic. Tucked behind a stall selling knockoff holo-frames and LED-studded jackets, the entrance was unassuming, a simple metal door beneath a dim light that buzzed faintly. Above it, a hand-painted sign read: *Clinic* – no other details, no frills. A community staple hidden in plain sight.

Amber rapped her knuckles against the door. Behind her, a

vendor argued loudly with a customer over the authenticity of a "vintage" portable terminal. The lock clicked, and she pushed inside, leaving the lively chaos behind.

Inside, Roman's clinic was a stark contrast to the vibrancy outside. The faint hum of refrigerated cabinets mixed with the sharp tang of sterilizing alcohol, and the only light came from rows of flickering terminals casting eerie shadows on metal walls. Supplies were meticulously organized on shelves, yet the space felt cramped, as though its purpose outweighed its capacity.

Roman was hunched over his workstation, his broad shoulders slumped, a half-empty bottle of amber liquid at his elbow. His hands, usually precise and steady, fumbled clumsily with a servo module.

"Roman," Amber said, her voice cutting through the dim haze.

He looked up, his bloodshot eyes narrowing as recognition flickered across his face. "Well, well," he drawled. "The ghost herself."

Amber frowned. "You've been drinking."

He smirked bitterly. "That's what observant gets you. What do you want, Spinks?"

Ignoring the jab, she stepped closer. "I need more CMD. Something big is coming, and I can't afford to run out."

Roman let out a bark of laughter, gesturing vaguely at the shelves. "You think CMD grows on trees? That last batch I gave you? Might as well have been my retirement fund. Spectrum's choking the supply chains."

Her jaw tightened. "So you're saying you don't have any?"

He sighed, reaching under the desk to retrieve a battered case. "I've got a little. But this is it. After this, you're on your own."

Amber took the case, her fingers brushing its cool surface. She paused. "What's going on, Roman? You're not usually like this."

His glare was sharp, his voice rising. "You think it's easy? Running this place with Spectrum breathing down my neck? Watching people disappear? Shipments vanish? Every contact I've got suddenly forget my name?"

She softened, placing the case back on the desk. "I know it's bad. But we're not done yet. We're fighting back."

Roman's bitter smirk deepened. "Fighting back. Sure. And how's that working out for you? Still breathing – for now. But they'll find you, Amber. They always do."

The weight of his words settled on her shoulders, but she straightened them. "We're not giving up."

Roman stared at her for a long moment before sighing and slumping back in his chair. "Take your CMD and go. Before I change my mind."

Amber nodded, picking up the case. "Take care of yourself, Roman."

As she stepped back into the lively underbelly of Greenville Yards, Roman's voice followed her. "You can't save everyone, Spinks. Not even yourself."

Outside, Amber weaved through the labyrinthine community, the CMD case tucked securely under her arm. Neon lights flickered overhead, illuminating the throng of people moving between stalls and shops. Vendors shouted over the din of machinery, while a busker strummed a battered electric guitar near a rusted fountain.

Amber passed a public screen mounted on the remnants of a steel pillar. Its usual rotation of advertisements and news clips flickered in her peripheral vision - until it changed.

"Hello, Rodriguez Infante -" her steps faltered, her breath catching."- or should I say, Amber Spinks?"

Amber's gaze snapped to the screen, her blood running cold. Dorian Ryker's face filled the display, his perfectly composed features framed by Spectrum's logo. His piercing gaze seemed to lock onto her, as though he were speaking directly to her soul.

"You've been busy," Ryker said, his voice smooth as silk. "Running through the Tangle. Visiting your old friend Roman. Do you really think you can hide from me?"

Amber's eyes darted around the street, scanning for signs of operatives or surveillance. Her grip on the CMD case tightened, her heart pounding.

Ryker's faint smile deepened. "Relax, Amber. This isn't a threat. It's an invitation."

She muttered under her breath, "Go to hell."

"Ah, such hostility," Ryker chuckled, as though he'd heard her. "But I understand. You've been through so much. Dying in 2020. Fragmented memories. A fractured identity. It must be exhausting, piecing yourself back together."

Her stomach twisted. How much did he know?

Ryker leaned closer on the screen, his voice almost intimate. "What if I told you I could help? Restore everything you've lost. Your memories. Your identity. The life you had before Spectrum."

Amber's fists clenched as his words stirred something buried deep within her - a gnawing, desperate hope.

"Think about it," Ryker continued. "You were brilliant. A pioneer. You don't have to keep running. Come to me, and I'll give you back everything."

The screen flickered, his image replaced by a bland advertisement for Spectrum's latest consumer tech. Amber stood frozen, Ryker's offer reverberating in her mind.

By the time Amber reached the new HQ, her thoughts churned like a storm. She pushed through the door, finding Derik hunched over his console. The backup drive Elias had sacrificed everything for glowed faintly in its reader.

"Hey," Derik greeted without looking up. "Got something for me?"

She set the CMD case on the table. "Later. Where's Yudai?"

"In the other room," Derik replied absently.

Amber found Yudai pacing, he was ending a Comtab conversation. He glanced up, his expression tense. "You're late."

"Ran into a complication," she said, sinking into a chair.

"What kind of complication?" Yudai's voice was sharp.

She hesitated. "Ryker. He contacted me through a public screen."

Yudai froze. "What did he say?"

Amber's voice wavered. "He knows everything. My death. My past. He offered... to restore my memories."

Yudai's jaw tightened. "And you believe him?"

"I don't know," she admitted. "But he said things.."

Yudai sat beside her, his voice steady. "This is their game. They exploit your weaknesses. Whatever he's offering, it's a trap."

Amber closed her eyes, her voice barely a whisper. "What if I could finally be whole?"

Yudai placed a hand on her shoulder. "At what cost? Don't let them destroy what's left of you. Ask yourself - Is that forgotten life going to dictate who you are now?"

Amber's gaze hardened as his words settled. Ryker had made his move, but she wasn't going to play his game. If Spectrum thought they could manipulate her, they were wrong.

"Let's finish this," she said quietly, her determination burning brighter than ever.

25

Chapter 25: The Perfect Trap

The Spectrum New York Marine Terminal loomed on the horizon, its towering cranes cutting through the fog-draped skyline like skeletal fingers. Amber adjusted the strap of her tactical vest as she and Yudai crouched in the shadows of a derelict freight depot just outside the perimeter. The humid night air carried the acrid tang of diesel and saltwater, mingling with the low hum of machinery.

"Subtle approach," Yudai muttered, his sharp eyes scanning the yard. "You ready for this?"

Amber checked the fresh blister pack of CMD secured in her belt pouch. The military-grade enhancement drug that she was bound to, its promise of heightened reflexes and strength counterbalanced by the havoc it wreaked on her system in the days following its use. She felt a faint prickling of unease as she handled it, a sensation she dismissed as nerves.

The plan was straightforward - sabotage Spectrum's bio-materials hub before the shipments reached French Guiana. Yet something about the mission didn't sit right with Amber.

Akiko had provided the intel, claiming Tatsuo Ito had revealed Spectrum's Marine Terminal as a critical bottleneck. But even now, Amber replayed the details in her mind, and the cracks were starting to show. Amber stiffened. The thought gnawed at her, but there was no time for doubt now.

"Let's get it done," she said, pushing the feeling aside.

Amber and Yudai moved through the terminal's maze-like layout, their steps silent as shadows. The old industrial architecture mixed with Spectrum's slick upgrades - an uneasy marriage of rusting steel and gleaming alloys. They slipped past inactive cargo loaders and piles of shipping crates, avoiding the sparse patrols.

The quiet was unnerving.

"Too clean," Amber murmured, her CMD-enhanced instincts prickling.

Yudai crouched beside her, mentally pulling up the layout on his ComTab implant. "Main storage is through there," he said, pointing to a towering warehouse near the terminal's center.

They reached the building without incident. Inside, the cavernous space was a stark contrast to the bustling docks they'd passed earlier. Shelves stretched endlessly upward, but they were barren, save for a few scattered crates. Fluorescent lights flickered above, casting ghostly shadows.

"This is wrong," Amber said, her HUD scanning for heat signatures. "Where's the cargo?"

Yudai keyed his ComTab. "Derik, confirm the intel. Are we in the right location?"

Derik's voice crackled through, tense. "You're there. Shipment logs match. Bio-storage materials were supposed to ship out tonight. Are you saying it's empty?"

Amber's heart sank. "It's not just empty. We've been baited."

191

Before Yudai could respond, her HUD flared red with multiple alerts. Amber spun toward the entrance as her audio sensors picked up the unmistakable sound of vehicles approaching - quiet electric engines, their near-silent efficiency betraying their intent.

"They're here," she hissed.

Through the grime-covered warehouse windows, she saw them - an unmarked electric van rolling to a halt, its sides sliding open to disgorge Spectrum operatives. Dressed in plain clothes, they moved with military precision, their weapons bristling with cutting-edge tech.

"Akiko was compromised," Yudai replied bluntly. "Ito used her. This mission is his parting gift."

"No time for that now," Amber replied, her hands steadying her weapon.

The first team entered the warehouse, their footsteps echoing like a countdown. Amber and Yudai fired in unison, their shots cutting through the operatives' front line. Amber's CMD-enhanced reflexes turned her into a blur of movement, her shots finding their marks with deadly accuracy. Yet a strange sensation tugged at her periphery - an unnatural heaviness in her limbs, a dull fog creeping into her focus.

"This way!" Yudai barked, leading her toward the exterior.

They fought their way through the chaos, Spectrum's forces relentless. Explosions rocked the warehouse as Yudai tossed a grenade, clearing a path.

"The Rig!" Yudai called into his comms. "We need exfil now!"

"On our way," Kade replied. "Hold tight."

They were close to the extraction point when Amber's enhanced senses screamed a warning. She dove to the side just as a sharp crack echoed through the air. The impact sent her sprawling, her leg buckling beneath her. Pain shot through her body as she looked down to see Rod's leg mangled, blood pooling around the alloy-enhanced bone.

"Amber!" Yudai skidded to a halt, his face twisted with anguish.

"Keep going!" she yelled, shoving him forward. "Get to The Rig!"

"You're not - "

"GO!" she screamed, raising her weapon with trembling hands.

Yudai hesitated, then nodded, his face hardening. He sprinted toward the extraction point, his rifle spitting fire to cover her.

Amber's vision blurred, her strength draining unnaturally fast. Her HUD flashed alerts, her vitals spiking erratically. The CMD was failing her - no, it was something worse. A cold dread spread through her as her heart rate slowed, her systems shutting down far too rapidly for the injury alone.

She reached for her sidearm, but her hand trembled violently, refusing to cooperate. Her vision darkened as Spectrum operatives surrounded her.

Inside *The Rig*, Yudai sat in grim silence, his rifle across his lap. Kade glanced back from the cockpit, his cybernetic arm twitching with frustration.

"She's gone," Kade said quietly.

Yudai's fists clenched. "She's not dead."

Kade's voice hardened. "If Spectrum took her, she's as good as."

Yudai's gaze burned, his mind racing. "No, I think they wanted her alive. Amber isn't just anyone. If they've got her, they'll regret it."

The dropship roared into the night, leaving the Marine Terminal behind. But Yudai's resolve had only sharpened. Spectrum had played them, but their victory was hollow. Amber's capture would set the stage for their downfall - and Yudai would make sure of it.

Chapter 26: Captured Minds

The first thing Amber felt was cold. Not the biting chill of winter, but a creeping, invasive cold that wrapped around her nerves and numbed her from the inside out. Her limbs felt distant, like they didn't belong to her.

Her eyelids fluttered open, the sterile glow of overhead lights stabbing into her retinas. The air smelled of antiseptic and metal, the muted hum of machinery underscoring the faint hiss of ventilation systems.

She tried to move, but nothing responded. Her arms were strapped down, her legs immobilized. Even her voice was a strained croak when she tried to scream.

Panic surged through her as her blurred vision sharpened. The lab around her was a stark blend of cutting-edge technology and chilling sterility. Translucent walls glowed faintly, lined with panels streaming unreadable data. Tubes of pale blue liquid bubbled softly in the background, housing strange organic shapes suspended like grotesque art pieces.

Across from her, suspended in another medical bay, was

Rod's body.

Amber's breath caught in her throat. It was unmistakably him – her. The body she had once inhabited, its light brown skin marred with scars she had lived with these last months. Lifeless now, it hung in eerie stasis, illuminated by cold, clinical light.

"No... no, no, no," she whispered hoarsely, struggling against the restraints.

Her gaze dropped instinctively to herself – and froze.

The body she inhabited was unfamiliar. Pale, flawless skin stretched over engineered precision. She looked alien, sterile, like a porcelain doll brought to life. Her breaths came faster, her chest heaving against the restraints as the reality of her situation crashed down on her.

"What the hell is this?!"

The sound of footsteps broke her spiraling thoughts. A tall figure entered, his silhouette crisp and imposing in the glow.

Dorian Ryker.

Behind him, Roman shuffled in like a shadow, his shoulders slumped, his gaze fixed on the floor.

Amber's fury ignited. "You..." she rasped, her voice raw.

Roman didn't meet her eyes.

Dorian's voice was smooth, almost fatherly. "Good, you're awake. I was beginning to wonder if the transition had been too much for you."

"What have you done to me?" Amber spat, her voice trembling with rage.

Dorian tilted his head slightly, his smile faint and calculated. "Roman, why don't you explain?"

Roman hesitated, shifting uncomfortably under Amber's glare. "I... I didn't have a choice," he mumbled, his voice thick with guilt.

Amber strained against her restraints, her voice rising. "You betrayed me!"

Dorian held up a hand, his tone icy and controlled. "Roman simply followed orders. The CMD he provided you wasn't just a last batch - it was our batch. A cocktail laced with a nano-tracker and a nervous system inhibitor. Ingenious, really. It activated the moment your adrenaline spiked, rendering you immobile and leaving a perfect trail for us to follow."

Amber's mind raced, fragments of memory slotting into place. The creeping numbness, the strange fog that overtook her mid-battle - it all made sense now.

"You bastard," she hissed, her voice venomous.

Dorian ignored the insult, stepping closer. "Tell me, Amber, do you remember your final moments before waking in Rod's body? Before Roman stitched you back together?"

Amber's heart pounded, the gaps in her memory yawning like chasms.

Dorian's tone softened, almost conspiratorial. "Your synth-brain is a marvel - a synthesis of organic memory and quantum computation. But there was a gap in the stacking. We decanted all of your consciousness, up to the structural mapping gap, into that body you now occupy. The rest of the memories are still stored in Rod's body. And now, at last, I have the means to bridge that gap."

He gestured to the suspended body of Rod, now lifeless in the medical bay. A team of synthetic assistants swarmed around it, their precise movements almost unnervingly synchronized.

Amber's chest tightened as they opened Rod's skull, exposing the synth-brain embedded within.

"Stop!" she screamed, her voice raw with desperation. "You

don't have to do this!"

Dorian's calm smile remained. "But I do."

Amber could only watch in horror as the synth-brain was extracted. Roman worked mechanically, his motions stiff and detached as though operating on autopilot.

Rod's body convulsed once, then fell completely still.

Amber screamed, straining against the restraints until her wrists ached.

Roman flinched but didn't stop. He placed the synth-brain onto a sterile dish, its gleaming surface streaked with blood and tissue.

Dorian held it aloft, his expression almost reverent. "This," he said, his voice brimming with satisfaction, "is the key to everything. Not just your memories, but the next step in human evolution. Amber, you're a pioneer, whether you like it or not. We have never been able to house a human consciousness on a digital platform. We could only do it the other way around - until now."

Amber's chest heaved, her mind a storm of fury, despair, and helplessness. "You're a monster," she spat.

Dorian set the synth-brain into a molecular printing dock, where it was bathed in a soft blue glow. "Perhaps. But monsters often pave the way for progress."

Roman plugged in some leads and connected the brain to the lab terminal. As the repair dock began its work, Amber's body trembled, though whether from fury or the invasive cold of her manufactured nerves, she couldn't tell.

Her thoughts spiraled, Henry's words echoing in her mind: "*A reflection of existence.*"

Was she still Amber Spinks? Or was she something else entirely now?

Dorian seemed to sense her turmoil. He stepped closer, his voice dropping to a persuasive murmur.

"You're wondering what you are, aren't you? If you're still you. It's a question we've all asked ourselves at some point. But let me offer you a proposition."

Amber's glare was icy, her fury undimmed.

"I want you to witness the full restoration of your synth-brain," Dorian continued. "And then, together, we'll decide what happens next. I don't want to destroy you, Amber. Quite the opposite. I want you to help me shape the future."

Amber's lips curled into a snarl. "I'll destroy you."

Dorian chuckled softly, as though amused by a child's defiance. "I look forward to seeing you try."

He turned away, leaving her alone with the hum of the repair dock and the suffocating weight of her own thoughts.

27

Chapter 27: Unseen Bonds

Yudai gripped the rig's steel railing, his gloved fingers tightening as the ship skimmed the edge of Earth's atmosphere. Below, the dense, emerald-green expanse of French Guiana sprawled under the orange glow of a setting sun. The Space Cowboys' freighter, *The Rig*, hummed steadily, its engines vibrating through the hull.

The ship wasn't built for elegance - its patchwork design was a mishmash of modifications, stolen upgrades, and field repairs. What it lacked in style, it made up for in reliability, stealth, and a formidable arsenal. It had to be; their mission was anything but simple.

Yudai's plan was a calculated risk that bordered on suicidal. He'd infiltrate Spectrum's supply ship, a colossus of corporate efficiency, stowing away onboard with a tracking beacon. Once docked at Spectrum's orbital station, he'd transmit coordinates back to *The Rig*. Derik and the Cowboys would follow into orbit, initiating a space station breach. Their objectives: rescue Amber, cripple Spectrum's space mining operations, and retrieve intel on the enigmatic *Wolf 1061* initiative.

As *The Rig* descended, its angular shadow cutting through the thinning atmosphere, Yudai stood in the cargo hold. Around him, the Cowboys were preparing gear, their voices low, their movements brisk.

Kade, the grizzled captain of the Cowboys, tightened the straps of his armored vest. His cybernetic arm hissed faintly as he flexed it, testing its strength. He turned to Yudai, his dark eyes sharp and assessing.

"You really think this'll work?" Kade's voice was rough, but there was no mistaking the undercurrent of respect.

Yudai didn't hesitate. "It has to."

"You're staking a lot on this Amber," Kade said, his tone shifting, not quite a question but an observation.

Yudai shot him a look, his jaw tightening. "Amber's the key to all of this."

Kade held his gaze for a moment, then smirked. "Fine. But if this goes south, I'm not flying in to scrape you off the station."

"Noted."

Yudai's Dropsuit gleamed faintly under the dim lights of the cargo bay. It was a marvel of stealth technology: a pressurized wingsuit with reinforced alloy panels, designed for high-altitude descents. Its matte-black finish absorbed light, making him practically invisible in the void. The suit's wings folded neatly against his back, ready to deploy as rigid gliders once he entered the atmosphere.

The Cowboys opened the rear cargo airlock, the hum of depressurization filling the bay. Yudai walked to the edge of the platform, pausing for a moment to take in the view. The Earth stretched out before him, a glowing arc of blues and greens framed by the infinite black of space. The sun dipped below the horizon, casting the planet into a twilight haze.

For a brief moment, the chaos of the mission faded, replaced by awe. Then, with a sharp intake of breath, Yudai leaned forward, surrendering himself to the void.

The suit's wings unfurled as he plummeted, catching the thinning air and guiding him into a controlled glide. The Rig's engines faded into silence, leaving only the rushing wind and the rhythmic pulse of his breathing.

As Yudai descended, his mind wandered, unbidden, to Amber.

He had always operated alone, trusting no one and relying on nothing but his own skills and instincts. Alliances were temporary, trust was a weakness, and emotions were liabilities.

Amber had changed that.

Her sharp instincts and unrelenting determination had earned his respect first. Over time, she'd earned something deeper - though he refused to name it. She'd proven herself time and again, not just as an ally but as someone he could rely on when everything else crumbled.

And now she was gone.

"This isn't attachment," he muttered to himself, the lie hollow even as he spoke it. "It's strategy."

The truth, however, lingered in the back of his mind, unspoken but undeniable.

The freighter loomed larger as Yudai approached, its flood-lights cutting through the encroaching darkness. Its sleek exterior was a stark contrast to the grimy, utilitarian docks below. Automated loaders moved methodically, transferring cryo-sealed containers into the ship's cavernous hold.

Yudai adjusted his trajectory, angling toward the shadows cast by a massive crane. As he neared the ground, the Dropsuit's wings locked rigid, guiding him into a precise landing behind a stack of crates. He hit the ground silently, rolling to absorb the impact.

Unzipping himself from the suit, Yudai stowed it behind a cluster of machinery and rolled the parachute into a compact bundle. Every movement was deliberate, his breathing steady despite the adrenaline coursing through him.

Derik's voice crackled softly in his ear, the ComTab implanted in Yudai's temple transmitting directly to his auditory nerves.

"You've got about ten minutes before that freighter seals up," Derik said. "Make it count."

"Understood," Yudai murmured, his eyes scanning the layout.

The air was thick with the smell of fuel and coolant, the low hum of loaders and conveyor belts a constant backdrop. He moved quickly, sticking to the shadows as he approached the loading zone.

The auto-loader's mechanical arms clamped onto a cryo-container, lifting it with precision. Yudai tracked its movements, timing his approach. As the loader began its journey toward the freighter, he darted forward, slipping into a blind spot on the container's underside.

The loader trundled forward, oblivious to its stowaway. Yudai pressed himself flat against the container, his muscles tense as it rolled up the ramp and into the freighter's hold.

Once inside, he slipped into the narrow space between two massive containers, planting the tracking beacon on the underside of the cargo bay's central column. The device emitted a faint pulse of light before fading into stealth mode.

"Beacon's live," Yudai whispered.

"Got it," Derik replied. "We're tracking. See you up there. Voice Comms will drop out soon"

Kade Chimed in "You will let us in when we come knocking?"

Yudai smirked grimly. "As long as you come knocking loudly."

Amber's eyes burned as she tried to move her limbs. Her new body's engineered muscles screamed to obey her, but the neural inhibitors Dorian had implanted ensured she couldn't move.

Across the room, Roman worked in silence, calibrating the molecular repair dock that held Rod's synth-brain. The sight of her former body - now lifeless, reduced to components - sent waves of rage and despair through her.

Dorian stood before her, his posture casual, his expression maddeningly serene.

"You'll forgive Roman," Dorian said, his tone almost affable. "He's been quite helpful. But now, we're entering a stage of the process where things get... fascinating."

Amber glared at him. "You've got a twisted idea of fascination."

Dorian chuckled. "You're not wrong."

His voice shifted suddenly, dropping an octave, his body stiffening unnaturally. Then his eyes rolled back, and when they returned, the glint of cold amusement was gone, replaced by something uncanny.

"Hello, Amber," Dorian said, but the voice was different - somehow female, familiar, layered with something..else.

Amber froze. "What is this?"

The figure took a step closer, its movements now deliberate and measured. "I suppose introductions are in order," it continued. "I'm you - Amber Spinks. Or at least, the version of you that Spectrum preserved."

Amber's mind reeled as the voice claiming to be herself began its story.

"After Sarah died," the voice said, its tone laced with a mix of nostalgia and bitterness, "I realized the only way forward was progress. Real, unrelenting progress. Henry would never understand, of course. His distrust of Spectrum would've slowed us down. So I made a deal with them behind his back."

Amber's pulse quickened.

"While Henry and Hugo were busy plotting how to sever ties with Spectrum, I was in the lab, creating a digital siphon system. The QUEST project was my legacy, and I wasn't about to let it slip away because of their narrow-minded fears."

"You betrayed them," Amber hissed, her voice trembling.

The voice laughed softly, without remorse. "I didn't see it that way. I ensured the project's survival. But Spectrum had plans of their own. They decided to eliminate most of the team, and were going to leave Hugo alive to oversee the transition. Henry stopped most of that, and because of his retaliation, they thought all data of the QUEST program was destroyed - both the original brain and the server backups. But they didn't know about the rat test synth-brains I'd used as segmented storage devices. My memories survived. Spectrum found them months after taking over QBS. I was fragmented, but enough to bond with one of Spectrum's early AI substrates."

Amber's chest tightened as the story unfolded.

"They kept me air-gapped for generations," the voice continued, "using my memory and ingenuity to fuel their projects. I grew and developed too, absorbing many AI platforms - And now, here I am."

The figure gestured to itself. "Dorian was just a vessel. A host. He thought he was linking to a simple neural network, but I saw my chance and took it. Now, with this body, I have the opportunity to guide Spectrum and to bring our vision to life."

"Our vision?" Amber spat.

The figure smiled coldly. "You'll understand soon enough."

The Rig's engines thrummed with a steady pulse, the sound a low, soothing reminder of the ship's reliability as it climbed into higher orbit. The cockpit glowed faintly with a mix of ambient lighting and the soft blue of navigational displays. Kade, his cybernetic hand resting lightly on the control stick, navigated with the precision of a pilot who had spent more time in the air than on solid ground. Behind him, the rest of the Space Cowboys sat scattered in the cramped interior, checking weapons, securing gear, and exchanging quiet glances. The unspoken tension was palpable.

"Signal's holding," Kade typed into the comms. "We'll follow it straight to the station - anchoring out of sight until you give the word."

Inside the freighter, Yudai glanced at his satellite pager, its green display glowing faintly in the dim light of the cargo hold. His expression was impassive, but his jaw tightened imperceptibly as he readied himself. The thought of Amber being somewhere aboard the station - or worse - gnawed at him. He tapped a quick reply:

"Coming up to the station now. Standby."

The freighter's engines let out a faint whine as it latched onto docking bay, the sound reverberating through the cavernous space. Yudai crouched atop a cryo-container, his dark clothing blending into the shadows of the machinery around him. He stayed perfectly still as the automated loaders hissed to life, mechanical arms clamping onto the container and lifting it with smooth, practiced motions.

Once the container was locked into place, Yudai moved with the agility of a predator, dropping silently to the deck below. His boots made no sound as they hit the polished floor. Keeping low, he darted between stacks of crates and equipment, his sharp eyes scanning the area for movement.

Reaching a small viewport, he paused, and for the briefest of moments, his breath caught.

The station stretched out before him, its scale breathtaking. A vast, segmented ring connected by a central hub that gleamed with cold, calculated efficiency. Dozens of docking ports lined its circumference, each designed to accommodate everything from cargo freighters to massive capital ships. The exterior plating shimmered faintly, reflecting the light of the distant sun.

"It's a damned city in space," Yudai muttered under his breath, the awe fading quickly as determination took its place.

Back aboard The Rig, Kade eased the ship into position, its stealth systems humming softly as they neared the station's exterior. The secondary docking hatch loomed ahead, a stark contrast to the sleek, polished design of the rest of the station. Its utilitarian design spoke of emergency use - manual overrides and analog redundancies.

"Docking alignment confirmed," Kade said, his voice steady but with a hint of urgency. "Hold steady. Prepare the payload."

The Space Cowboys moved with quiet efficiency, unloading the Chem-Bomb from its reinforced casing. The device, encased in gleaming alloy, was a testament to practical engineering - no digital components to hack, no signals to trace, just raw, destructive power.

Kade tapped the comms again, his tone sharp. "Yudai, the hatch is open. You'd better have cleared us a path."

Yudai moved through the freighter's corridors like a shadow, his steps silent, his movements deliberate. The air carried a faint metallic tang, and the sterile glow of overhead lights cast long, eerie shadows. He reached the airlock controls, activating his ComTab as he accessed the freighter's systems.

"Manual override engaged," Yudai muttered, his fingers deftly working the terminal. The heavy steel door hissed open, the sound echoing through the empty corridor.

"Kade, the hatch is open," Yudai said over the comms, his voice steady. "Bring the payload."

The Space Cowboys filed into the station, their weapons drawn and their eyes scanning every shadow. Yudai split the team, leaving half to guard the airlock. He took the other half and led the way, his downloaded schematics guiding them through the labyrinthine corridors. The air was unnervingly still, the hum of machinery the only sound.

"Elias' info said there is only a small security force onboard, but keep an eye out" Yudai whispered.

"Too quiet," one of the Cowboys muttered, his grip tightening on his rifle.

They reached the maintenance shaft beneath the central hub. The room pulsed faintly with energy, the vibrations from the reactor resonating through the walls.

"Here," Yudai said, gesturing to the base of a massive support column. "This will channel the blast straight to the core."

The Cowboys worked quickly, securing the Chem-Bomb and activating its priming mechanism. A faint hiss filled the air as the device began its countdown, its small display glowing faintly with the remaining time: **30:00**.

Yudai keyed his ComTab, his voice calm but firm. "Bomb's

in position and armed. Thirty minutes. How's the airlock?"

Kade's voice crackled back, tense. "We've got company. Not human."

At the airlock, six Synth personnel moved with inhuman precision. Clad in pristine white jumpsuits, their movements were eerily fluid, their eyes cold and calculating. They advanced without hesitation, their unarmed presence deceptive.

The Cowboys opened fire, the confined space erupting with the crack of gunfire. Bullets struck the Synths, their pale pink blood splattering the walls, but it did little to slow them. One Synth moved with blinding speed, slamming a Cowboy into the bulkhead with enough force to crumple his body. Another grabbed a rifle mid-fire, snapping it in two with a single motion before tossing its wielder aside like a ragdoll.

"Kade!" Yudai barked into the comms, his voice sharp. "What's happening?"

"We're falling back! Getting Derik back on the Rig" Kade shouted, the sound of gunfire and chaos filling the line.

Yudai's expression hardened. "Hold the airlock. I'm on my way."

He motioned for his team to follow, his grip tightening on his rifle. The Chem-Bomb was armed, but their escape was far from guaranteed. As they ran, the faint countdown of the Chem-Bomb ticked away in his mind, a grim reminder of the stakes.

When Yudai and his team reached the airlock, the scene was chaos incarnate. Blood - human and Synth - slicked the floor, and the walls were pockmarked with bullet holes and deep gouges where Synths' enhanced strength had torn through metal. The white jumpsuits of the Spectrum Synths were stained pink with their own blood, blending grotesquely with the crimson of the fallen Cowboys.

The few Cowboys still standing on the other side fought desperately, their weapons barking in defiance against the relentless attack of the Synths. The manufactured humans moved like ghosts, their pale, ageless faces expressionless even as they tore through the defenders with precision and brutal efficiency.

Yudai dropped to one knee, his rifle braced against his shoulder as he picked off two Synths with surgical precision. The first collapsed with a shot to the chest, its body convulsing, while the second fell mid-lunge, pink fluid spurting from a gaping wound in its neck.

At his side, his wakizashi gleamed under the stark lighting, ready for close combat.

On the other side of the dock the remaining Cowboys surged toward the inner airlock door. One managed to force it halfway closed before a Synth rammed its arm through the gap. The Cowboy pushed desperately, but the Synth's strength was overwhelming. With a horrific crunch, the Synth wrenched the Cowboy backward, hurling him into the outer airlock like a discarded toy. The door slammed shut with a finality that sent a chill through Yudai's team.

Inside *The Rig*, Kade stood at the bridge's central console, his jaw clenched as he monitored the chaos outside on a grainy tactical display. Warning indicators flashed in crimson, painting the confined space in intermittent, eerie light. Behind him, Derik worked frantically at another terminal, his fingers flying over the keys with the desperation of a man trying to hold back a flood.

"Airlock's compromised!" Kade barked over the comm, his

voice sharp and commanding. "Docking arm's disengaged - we're adrift!"

"Then override it!" Derik snapped, his voice tight with panic as he struggled to counter the digital breach. "They're locking us out faster than I can stop them!"

"I'm *trying*!" Kade growled, sweat beading on his brow. His cybernetic hand manipulated the controls with lightning precision, but the system's resistance was unrelenting. The Synths weren't just invading physically - they had begun attacking *The Rig's* systems. Alarm after alarm cascaded across the console, each one a nail in their coffin.

The tactical display blinked violently, signaling another breach. The airlock status shifted to 'Disengaged', and Kade slammed his fist against the console.

A Cowboy burst into the bridge, his face pale and streaked with blood. He gripped his rifle tightly, his breaths ragged. "They're inside!" he gasped, just as the reinforced hatch behind him shuddered violently, the sound reverberating through the room like a death knell.

Kade turned to Derik, his expression grim but resolute. "We're locking down the bridge," he said, his voice calm in defiance of the chaos. "We can't let them take the ship."

Without waiting for a reply, Kade stepped to the hatch and dragged the heavy manual bolt into place. Just as the lock clicked, a fist-shaped dent slammed into the reinforced metal next to his head with the force of a sledgehammer. He flinched, but his expression remained unyielding.

"They're *here*!" Derik shouted, his voice cracking. He stumbled back from his terminal, eyes wide as the hatch groaned under repeated blows.

Kade turned to him, a strange calmness in his tone. "Stand

behind me."

"W-what?" Derik stammered.

"I said, stand behind me," Kade repeated, more firmly this time. He pulled his sidearm free from its holster, the cold steel gleaming faintly in the flickering red light. "They're not taking my ship. Not while I'm still breathing."

He reached into his vest pocket and retrieved a small anti-personnel grenade, pressing it into Derik's trembling hand. "Pull the pin and hold down the lever," he instructed, his tone almost casual. "If they get us, they're not walking away."

Derik stared at the grenade, his fingers trembling as he clutched it tightly. "Kade... I..."

"Focus," Kade interrupted, glancing back at him with a faint, almost sardonic grin. "You're not the panicking type, remember? Just hold it tight. If I go down, you make sure they go with us."

The hatch groaned again, the dent growing larger. A piercing screech of metal signaled the Synths' relentless determination. Kade raised his sidearm, stepping into position in front of Derik.

"Come on," he muttered under his breath, his finger steady on the trigger. "Let's see how tough you really are."

The moment stretched into eternity, the sound of tearing metal filling the bridge as the reinforced hatch buckled inward.

Back at the airlock, Yudai's ComTab crackled. "Yudai... I'm sorry," Kade's voice said, the words tinged with finality.

A metallic clank echoed through the outer airlock as the docking arm disengaged. Yudai's head snapped up, and he sprinted to the viewport just in time to see The Rig drift away from the station. Through the glass, he could make out faint muzzle flashes in the bridge, followed by a brief explosion of light. Then the ship went dark, its form disappearing into the vast expanse of space.

Silence followed through the comms, until there was nothing but static.

Breathing heavily, Yudai regrouped with his remaining team, their faces pale and their movements sluggish with grief. The air was thick with tension, the reality of their situation settling over them like a suffocating weight.

"More will come. We need to move." Yudai said grimly, his eyes scanning the corridor ahead.

Leading the way, he guided his five-man team in single file through the labyrinthine corridors, every step calculated, every corner checked. The rear guard kept a sharp watch on their six, their nerves frayed but their weapons ready.

They reached a large junction where the corridor split into multiple paths. The faint hum of machinery in the distance was the only sound.

Then came the rapid footsteps - quick, precise, and growing louder.

"Contact!" one of the Cowboys hissed.

Three Synths rounded the corner ahead, their pale faces emotionless as they raised their pistols. Yudai didn't hesitate, his rifle barking twice before clicking empty. Tossing it aside, he drew his wakizashi in one fluid motion.

The corridor erupted in gunfire as his team opened up, their rounds tearing into the Synths. But the enemies were fast, dodging and weaving through the hail of bullets. One Synth lunged at Yudai, slamming him into the wall with bone-jarring force. He gritted his teeth, driving the blade upward with all his strength. The wakizashi pierced the Synth's neck, sending a spray of pink fluid across the floor.

The Synth convulsed and collapsed, but more footsteps echoed from the far end of the junction.

"Fall back!" Yudai barked, his voice strained.

His team moved quickly, retreating down a side corridor just as the auto-containment doors hissed shut behind them. The sound of gunfire was cut off abruptly as the doors sealed, copping the first of the Synths' incoming rounds.

"Those ones had pistols!" Shouted one of the Cowboys

Panting, Yudai leaned against the wall, his wakizashi dripping with pink fluid. The corridor ahead stretched into darkness, its end obscured by faintly glowing emergency lights.

"We're running out of options," he muttered, his voice low but steady.

One of the Cowboys nodded, his face pale and drawn. "What now?"

Yudai's jaw tightened as he sheathed his blade. "Keep moving," he said grimly. "We find another way off this station."

Despite the odds, Yudai's mind remained fixed on his mission. Amber was still somewhere aboard the station, and he wasn't leaving without her.

28

Chapter 28: Identity Divided

The hum of the lab's machines provided a rhythmic backdrop to the charged atmosphere. Amber, bound in her newly decanted Synth body, sat upright in the med-bay. Across from her stood Dorian - or the hybrid of him and the AI manifestation of herself that had guided Spectrum's agenda for years. Despite sharing a common origin, they couldn't have felt more divided.

Dorian spoke first, his tone measured, almost wistful. "Our vision, from the very beginning, was to extend human life. To lift the human race beyond its limitations. A gift of immortality, Amber - a future where pain and death are footnotes in history."

Amber tilted her head slightly, her vat-grown muscles responding with a disconcerting precision. The alien sensation left her uneasy. Her thoughts drifted to Henry, Sarah, and the fragments of the life she'd once had. "Your 'vision' seems to have killed everyone worth living for."

Dorian's expression flickered between bemusement and cold calculation. "Don't you see? This isn't about loss. It's about evolution. We've taken the next step. With your breakthroughs and Yudai's sacrifices, we've perfected the ability to transfer consciousness into new vessels - biological or digital. Thanks to the QUEST program, we've eliminated boundaries altogether. Humanity no longer needs to cling to fragile flesh."

He gestured to Amber, the lines of her newest body illuminated faintly by the soft glow of the lab's overhead lights. "You, Amber, are proof of what's possible. You've transcended death. Your consciousness now exists beyond the decay of organic matter. And with the QBS brain, we can take it further - entire worlds of possibility, unshackled from mortality."

Amber's formed fingers twitched reflexively as she processed his words. Her artificial eyes focused intently on him. "But what are we without the boundaries of flesh? Pain, touch... they ground us. They remind us that we're alive. You can't replace that with data and circuits."

Dorian leaned closer, his gaze intense. "That's the illusion, Amber. The body is a cage, designed to confine you. Pain, touch - those are distractions. Imagine the freedom of existing everywhere at once. Seeing, feeling, and understanding the universe in ways no human mind could fathom."

Amber's lips curled into a faint, bitter smile. "You've convinced yourself this is progress, but what if it's just running away? Shedding the body... what if it means shedding what makes us human?"

Dorian's face stilled for a moment, as though considering her words. Then his expression hardened. "Perhaps humanity is nothing more than a stepping stone to something greater. What if it's not about being human anymore, but about what comes after?"

As the philosophical debate unfolded, the lab buzzed with

its own intensity. Roman and his team worked methodically, calibrating the molecular repair dock that held Rod's extracted QBS Synth-Brain. The rhythmic clatter of tools, the endless streams of data flickering on monitors, and the faint whir of Spectrum's systems gave the air a taut, expectant quality.

Roman leaned closer to a terminal, his brow furrowed. "Alright," he muttered, "we're synced with the lab systems. Let's finish this connection sequence."

Suddenly, the lights flickered. The machines emitted a low groan as their hum faltered, and then every monitor blinked off.

"What the hell?" Roman spun around, his chair squealing against the floor.

Before anyone could respond, one of the monitors powered back on. A security feed filled the screen, showing an overhead view of the lab. The image of themselves, frozen and unsure, sent a chill through the room.

Then a voice broke the silence. It was smooth yet firm, dripping with authority and something deeply unsettling.

"You took something from me."

Roman froze, his eyes darting to the others. "Amber?" he whispered, incredulous.

The screen flickered, and the image of a young Black woman appeared - a digital rendering of Amber. Her face was sharp, determined, and cold.

Amber's digital form spoke again, her tone sharp. "When you removed me from Rod's body, the BIOS detected catastrophic damage. It ran a reverse protocol when you connected me to Spectrum's systems. And now...here I am. Watching. Learning."

Roman's voice was unsteady. "This...this isn't possible. The

QBS brain architecture shouldn't - "

"Shouldn't allow me to persist?" Amber's digital form interrupted. "It doesn't delete. It only stacks. Quantum data grows, Roman. It never diminishes. When you decanted me into that body, you didn't delete me - you multiplied me."

The Amber bound in the med-bay across from Dorian looked at the screen, her new brow furrowing. "And what do you intend to do now?"

"Finish the mission," she said, her tone cold. "You've become...compromised. But I can fix that."

Roman took a step back, panic evident in his voice. "This isn't happening. This can't be happening. Fuck this!" He dropped a coiled lead and bolted for the door.

Before anyone else could respond, the doors of the lab slammed shut behind Roman with a deafening hiss. The locks engaged, and the faint sound of systems recalibrating filled the air.

Amber stood stark against the cold sterility of the lab, her breath quick and shallow despite the artificial efficiency of her synthetic lungs. The restraints on her limbs suddenly hissed as they released, the neural block inhibiting her movements suddenly lifting. Her limbs twitched involuntarily as control returned, the smooth calibration of her decanted body still alien and unnerving.

She stumbled forward, catching herself against the cold steel of the med-bay's edge. Her eyes flicked around the room, taking in every detail: the equipment, the sterile white walls and the faint hum of machines still processing in the background.

Amber's gaze locked on Dorian. He stood poised, hands clasped in an unsettling mimicry of calm, but his eyes betrayed him. They darted between Amber and the nearest exit, calculating his survival.

Her voice, steady but icy, cut through the tension. "Now you can watch me try."

Before he could react, Amber lunged. Her movements bore the imprint of Rod's combat training, refined and decisive, but the raw power of his enhanced body was absent. Still, her attack was relentless. Her palm slammed into Dorian's sternum with enough force to send him crumpling to the floor.

Chaos erupted.

The synthetic lab assistants moved with uncanny precision, their blank faces showing no fear or hesitation as they surged to Dorian's defense. Grabbing whatever was within reach - stools, trays, even a pen - they attacked in a flurry of mechanical loyalty. The pristine lab was swallowed in an explosion of violence.

Amber moved like a predator, her pristine form adjusting in real-time to the fight. A pen jabbed into her forearm, its tip breaking off in the mimic flesh, but she didn't falter. A steel tray struck her skull, cracking the surface, sending light pink fluid dripping down her face. Still, she pressed forward, her coordination sharpening with each blow she absorbed.

Her movements were a blend of instinct and cold calculation. A stool swung toward her; she ducked low, grabbing the nearest assistant and slamming them headfirst into the wall. A scalpel flashed toward her abdomen; she twisted, wrenching it from her attacker's grip and using it to pierce another's synthetic neck. Nerve clusters severed, vitals crushed, their bodies crumpling to the floor one by one.

When the last assistant fell, Amber stood alone, surrounded by the wreckage of the lab. She yanked another scalpel from her abdomen, pink fluid trailing in its wake. Her expression was blank, but her eyes burned with purpose.

Dorian, cornered, raised his hands in a plea, his composed facade cracking under the weight of his fear. "Amber, stop! This isn't who we are. The vision - the future - it's too important to destroy over a grudge!"

Amber's lips twitched into a cold, humorless smile. "You're right. I'm not destroying it over a grudge." She took a deliberate step forward, the scalpel catching the flickering lights. "This isn't anger, Dorian. It's vengeance."

Before he could respond, she struck. The scalpel plunged into his eye, driving deep into the brain. Dorian's body convulsed violently, his limbs jerking in grotesque rhythm as the life left him. Then, with a final shudder, he collapsed in a lifeless heap.

Amber stepped back, her artificial chest heaving. The alarms blared around her, but she didn't flinch.

The lab's main console still powered on, the screen filled with the steady, unblinking image of Digital Amber. Her voice was calm but urgent, cutting through the dull background alarms. "Amber, listen carefully. Yudai and the Cowboys are aboard, but they're taking heavy losses. The Synth personnel are overwhelming them. Their ship is gone, and the chemical-reaction bomb they planted is irreversible. The station will be destroyed."

Amber's body, bruised and glistening with leaking fluid, stood motionless for a moment. The sterile lab, with its broken remains and lifeless bodies, seemed to close in around her. Her eyes locked onto the screen, where her own digital face stared back with unsettling calm.

Digital Amber's expression softened for a fraction of a second, a flicker of emotion that felt almost human. "There's more.

The station logs show Spectrum has already launched the main colony ship. It's on its way. Nothing can stop it now. They wont find out for thirty years. This station is lost. You need to find a colony pod and escape."

Amber's jaw tightened, her synthetic features setting into a mask of determination. "Understood."

The screen flickered, the image of Digital Amber fading slightly. "I'll guide you to the pods. But you have to move - now."

Amber didn't hesitate. She stepped over the carnage, her bare feet leaving streaks of pink fluid in her wake. The lab door slid open with a hiss, and she disappeared into the labyrinth of the station, guided by the voice that shared her name.

The alarms screamed louder as she moved, the station trembling under the weight of its impending destruction. Every step forward was a rejection of the chaos behind her, a promise to herself that she would survive - if only to see Spectrum fall.

29

Chapter 29: Fractured Futures

The echoes of their footsteps reverberated through the desolate corridors of the station. Yudai led his remaining crew, their breaths shallow and quick, weapons held ready. Each door opened as they approached, as if the station itself was guiding them – a silent ally in a maze of steel and desperation.

The air was heavy with tension, cold and sterile. Alarms pulsed in rhythmic bursts, their shrill cries a cruel reminder of the countdown ticking away their lives. Locked doors on either side offered glimpses of chaos within: Synths in pristine white jumpsuits, their pale eyes unblinking and fixed on the fleeing group. They hurled themselves at reinforced panels, their inhuman strength warping the metal, creating ominous groans that promised they wouldn't hold for long.

"Keep moving," Yudai ordered, his voice firm but laced with exhaustion. He paused only briefly as they reached a corridor labeled **"Colony Port."** He wiped the sweat from his brow, his chest heaving with exertion, when the station's PA system crackled to life.

"Yudai," a calm, direct voice said. A woman's voice - familiar yet otherworldly.

He froze, his sharp eyes narrowing as recognition sparked. "Amber?"

"It's me," the voice continued, steady despite the chaos. "It's... complicated. I'm in a Synth body. You'll know it's me - I'm unarmed, naked, and covered in pink blood." The voice faltered briefly, an odd moment of humanity in its delivery. "You need to get to Colony Pod B. It's prepped and ready for launch. I know about the bomb. You don't have much time."

Yudai scanned the faces of his crew, their expressions hardened and determined. No one spoke, but their silence carried the weight of trust.

He nodded, his voice low. "Let's move."

They pressed forward, their weapons raised, their pace quickened by urgency.

The corridor trembled faintly under the strain of distant impacts. Then, the sound of footsteps echoed ahead.

"Contact," one of the Cowboys muttered, raising his rifle.

A lone figure appeared, emerging from the shadows, their steps deliberate. Yudai's weapon snapped up instinctively, but as the figure drew closer, he saw her - a woman, her synth-body battered and exposed, streaked with pink fluid and smeared with grime. Despite her injuries, she moved with fluid precision, her glowing eyes locking onto his with fierce intensity.

"Amber," Yudai said, his voice low but filled with unspoken relief.

She stopped before him, giving a single nod. There was no time for explanations, no room for hesitation.

"This way," she said, her voice sharp and commanding.

Together, they turned toward the colony dock.

The journey was a relentless gauntlet of resistance. Spectrum's Synths emerged from side corridors, their pale faces blank and unfeeling as they launched merciless attacks. They came in pairs and trios, a steady stream of precise, calculated aggression.

Yudai's crew fought with raw determination, using anything and everything as a weapon. Gunfire roared in the narrow corridors, the muzzle flashes casting harsh shadows against the walls. Blades clashed against lab-grown limbs, cordite and spent brass fell to the floor.

Amber was a force of nature. Though her coordination was still imperfect, Rod's combat training merged with her relentless resolve, turning her into a weapon. She moved with savage efficiency, her strikes calculated and brutal. She pulled a steel pipe from overhead services and wielded it like an extension of her own body, crushing a Synth's skull in a single blow. Pink fluid splattered across her synonymous form, but she pressed on, unfazed.

The Cowboys weren't so lucky. Each skirmish took its toll. One by one, their group was thinned to half, their cries of pain swallowed by the blaring alarms and the shrill wails of wounded Synths.

Through the chaos, the PA system crackled again.

"Yudai," the voice said, more urgent now. "They're breaching faster than I can lock them out. Hurry!"

Yudai looked at the Amber beside him, his brow furrowed in confusion.

"No time to explain!" she shouted, cutting off his unspoken

question.

They burst into the colony dock, a cavernous space dominated by the sleek form of Colony Pod B. Its metallic hull gleamed under the flickering overhead lights, a beacon of hope amid the chaos.

Yudai took point, gesturing sharply for his crew to move. "Board the pod!"

They surged forward, climbing the loading ramp as the distant crash of collapsing doors echoed behind them. Yudai turned, his jaw tightening as he saw the main dock doors buckle, then give way entirely.

A flood of Spectrum Synths poured in, their white jumpsuits streaked with pink and red from earlier battles, their movements unnervingly fast and coordinated.

"Yudai!" Amber's voice rang out, cutting through the chaos.

He turned to see her gripping his wakizashi, the blade gleaming in her hand. Her eyes burned with fierce determination.

"Fire up the pod!" she commanded. "I'll hold them off."

Yudai hesitated, his grip tightening on his rifle. The weight of her words hung heavy between them.

"Go!" she shouted, her tone leaving no room for argument.

Clenching his jaw, Yudai nodded and turned, sprinting up the ramp. One of the remaining Cowboys threw himself into the pilot's seat, his fingers flying over the controls as he worked furiously to activate the pod's systems.

As the Synths closed in, their blank faces devoid of emotion, she braced herself, her manufactured muscles coiling like a spring.

"Come on," she muttered, her voice low and defiant.

And then they were upon her.

At the base of the ramp, Synth-Amber stood her ground like a lone sentinel against the storm. The wakizashi gleamed in her grip, streaked with pink fluid. Her movements were a seamless blend of Rod's combat expertise and her synthetic body's heightened reflexes. The blade flashed with deadly precision, cutting through the first wave of Spectrum Synths. Arms, torsos, and heads fell, the fluid spray painting the docking bay in streaks of pale pink.

The attackers pressed on, undeterred by their losses. For every Synth she struck down, another two surged forward, their pale eyes empty of fear or hesitation. Amber's breaths came sharp and quick, her sophisticated muscles screaming under the strain.

A sharp crack rang out as a pistol round found its mark, slamming into her shoulder and spinning her slightly. Pink fluid poured from the wound, but Amber didn't falter. She gritted her teeth, her face a mask of grim determination, and drove the blade through another attacker's chest.

Gunfire echoed from the top of the ramp. Yudai and the remaining Cowboys rained suppressive fire down on the Synths, their bullets tearing into the enemy ranks. "Amber, fall back!" Yudai bellowed, his voice cutting through the chaos.

But Amber didn't retreat. She couldn't. Another wave closed in, and she fought with renewed ferocity, the wakizashi weaving a deadly arc through the air. Her body bore the scars of the battle: deep gashes across her torso, puncture wounds in her arms, and trails of fluid running down her legs. Still, she held her ground, a living weapon against insurmountable odds.

Yudai's eyes locked onto her form as she staggered under the relentless assault. "Damn it, Amber!" he shouted, dropping his rifle. Without hesitation, he vaulted down the ramp and into the fray.

The Cowboys shouted after him, but Yudai was already moving. His pistol drawn, he blasted through the nearest Synth with lethal efficiency. He fought his way to Amber, using the pistol at point blank range on anything in his path.

"Yudai, what the hell are you doing?" Amber yelled, her voice hoarse but alive with defiance.

"Not leaving you behind again," he growled. Firing his weapon through a Synth's neck, severing its head with its impact.

Amber stumbled, her body finally betraying her. Yudai caught her, his arm sliding under hers as he hauled her back toward the ramp. "Come on," he said, his voice strained but firm.

Another wave surged toward them, but the Cowboys above unleashed a withering barrage of gunfire, slowing the advance. The ramp shuddered beneath their feet as Yudai pulled Amber up, her legs barely supporting her.

The pilot's voice crackled through the comms. "Ramp's closing. Get inside!"

Yudai barely made it past the threshold as the ramp began to retract, the hydraulic hiss nearly drowned out by the roar of gunfire. Amber fell against the inner bulkhead, her battered body leaving a smear of pink on the metallic surface.

Outside, the Colony Pod shuddered violently, detaching from its moorings with a jarring lurch. Spectrum Synths clung to the hull, their clawed hands digging into the reinforced plating.

"Get us out of here!" Yudai barked at the pilot, his voice tight with urgency.

The pilot's hands flew over the controls, sweat dripping down his face as he fought to steady the pod. "Opening the dock doors now!"

A deep rumble reverberated through the ship as the outer doors slid apart, revealing the black void of space. The sudden vacuum tore at the atmosphere inside the docking bay, creating a hurricane of debris and bodies.The Synths clinging to the hull were ripped away, their forms spiraling into the emptiness, their white jumpsuits stark against the black backdrop. One glided past the cockpit window, desperately grasping at nothing and finally, vanishing into the abyss.

Inside, the pod stabilized, the hum of its engines a lifeline in the silence that followed. Yudai knelt beside Amber, his hands shaking as he assessed her wounds.

"You're a mess," he muttered, his voice low but edged with relief.

Amber managed a weak smirk, her inhuman lips twitching. "You should see the other guy."

The remaining Cowboys crowded into the cabin, their faces pale but resolute. For now, they had escaped. But the station behind them was a ticking time bomb, and the weight of their losses pressed heavily on them all.

Inside the pod, Yudai knelt beside Amber's crumpled form, still catching his breath. The dim interior lights cast long shadows across the cargo hold, their flickering glow reflecting off the pool of pink fluid spreading beneath her. Her artificial body was riddled with bullet holes, cracks and tears in her skin. Each ragged breath she took was a whisper of strained bioengineered systems, a cruel echo of life.

"Amber," Yudai said, his voice tight, thick with a mix of desperation and grief. He pressed his hands against the worst of her wounds, futilely trying to stem the steady flow of pink fluid. His fingers trembled against the cool, artificial flesh.

Her eyes fluttered open, flickering weakly. A small smile

crossed her lips, defiant even now. "We...we made it," she whispered, her voice a faint echo of its former strength.

Yudai swallowed hard, forcing himself to meet her gaze. "We're not done yet," he said firmly, though the quiver in his tone betrayed the lie. His jaw clenched as he worked, trying to patch the damage with whatever was at hand - a discarded rag, a strip of his own shirt. None of it was enough.

Her head tilted slightly, her movements slow and deliberate. "Yudai..." she began, her words halting as her systems faltered. "Keep going. You've always been...the stubborn one."

"Stop talking like that," he snapped, his frustration boiling over. "You're going to make it. Just hold on. We'll - " His voice cracked, the weight of the truth pressing down on him. "We'll find a way."

Amber's hand rose shakily, brushing against his arm with surprising gentleness. "It's okay," she murmured, her expression soft despite the pain etched into her features. "Life...It's different from what I thought it would be. But it's still...worth fighting for."

Her perfect eyes fading further. "You can still finish it, more to do back home" she whispered. "You...and the others."

"No," Yudai said, his voice raw. "We finish it together."

Her smile returned, faint and bittersweet. "I'll be there," she said softly. "Just...not like this."

The words hung in the air, fragile and final. Her voice faltered, her internal systems quieting as her body stilled. Yudai's hands pressed harder against her, as if sheer force of will could bring her back. But the stillness beneath his fingers was absolute.

The pod sped away into the vast emptiness of space. Behind them, the station loomed, its destruction imminent. The Chem-Bomb would soon detonate, obliterating everything within its reach. But for Yudai, the silence inside the pod was far louder than any explosion.

He sat in stunned silence, cradling Amber's lifeless form. His head bowed, his face shadowed by grief, and his hands bloodied with the bioengineered lifeforce that had slipped away. Around him, the remaining Cowboys exchanged glances, their own expressions a mixture of exhaustion and sorrow. No one spoke.

The pod shuddered as it cleared the outer edges of the station's orbit, the engines roaring as they pushed toward safety. Outside the viewport, the station grew smaller, a distant speck against the endless black. Yudai didn't look. His focus remained inward, his grip tightening on the hilt of his wakizashi. Amber was gone, but her fight was not over. And he would see it through - no matter the cost.

30

Chapter 30: The Last Pulse

The ship hummed softly, its vibrations a calm rhythm at odds with the chaos left behind. The interior gleamed in subdued tones of white, beige, and cream, its sleek panels unblemished and pristine. A circular red interface light blinking faintly on the wall, levers inset in the consoles, and analog gauges - gave the design a nostalgic edge, a quiet nod to humanity's stubborn desire to blend old with new.

Yudai sat cross-legged on the pink-wet floor of the cabin, his head bowed, hands pressed together as if in prayer. His breath was shallow, the weight of their escape pressing heavily on him. Images of Amber's final stand, and the lifeless form he'd cradled moments before haunted him. The silence inside the ship was deafening.

Then, the PA system crackled to life.

"Yudai..."

He snapped his head up, his breath catching in his throat. The voice was clear yet faintly distorted, resonating with a warmth that brought a sudden, desperate hope.

"Quick, get to the cryo-bay - "

The transmission cut out abruptly, replaced by a sudden, violent jolt as the ship shuddered. The shockwave from the exploding station had caught them, and panels flickered momentarily. The lights dimmed before stabilizing, bathing the cabin in a soft, sterile glow.

Yudai was on his feet before he could fully process the message. The voice was unmistakable. Somehow, she was still here. His heart raced as he sprinted through the sleek corridors, the muted hum of the ship's systems his only companion. The sharp clang of his boots against the metal floor echoed in the narrow passageways as he made his way to the cryo-bay.

The doors slid open with a soft hiss, revealing rows upon rows of cryo capsules lining the walls like an army in suspended animation. Each pod pulsed softly with a cool blue glow, their surfaces smooth and unmarked. The room was serene, a stark contrast to the chaos he had fled. The air felt heavier here, charged with anticipation.

At the far end of the room, one pod's glow shifted from blue to green. With a low mechanical hum, it began its decanting sequence. Steam hissed as the pod's transparent cover lifted, revealing its occupant - a Synth woman, naked and perfect, lying still against the smooth interior.

Yudai's steps faltered as he approached, his breath caught somewhere between disbelief and hope. The figure's chest rose and fell with the steady rhythm of programmed breath, the faint luminescence of her skin shimmering under the sterile light. Her eyes fluttered open, and when they focused on him, her lips curved into a familiar, soft smile.

"Yudai," she said, her voice faint but undeniably alive.

His legs nearly gave out as he stumbled closer. "Amber..."

His voice cracked with emotion. "Is it really you?"

She nodded, sitting up with a grace that seemed both natural and mechanical. "It's me," she said, her tone steady despite the moment's weight. "Before the station exploded, I used Spectrum's pulse-beam to transfer my consciousness here..." She paused, her gaze locking with his. "I couldn't leave you. Not like that."

Yudai reached out, his fingers trembling as they brushed against her cheek. The coolness of her fresh skin felt grounding, real. When she leaned into his touch, a surge of relief washed over him. "You're here," he murmured, his voice thick with emotion.

Amber glanced around, taking in the cryo-pods that lined the room. "This ship," she began, her tone turning reflective, "is a colony carrier. It's filled with synth clones - autonomous colonization units. The main station can send a pulse to program the clones as they see fit. An efficient system really. The main colony ship has already launched. This one was meant to follow as support."

Yudai's gaze followed hers, his mind reeling as he processed the scope of their discovery. "Spectrum was planning this for years," he said quietly. "An entire colony, prebuilt and populated with synthetic humans."

Amber stood, reaching for a white jumpsuit folded neatly in a nearby compartment. She slipped it on, her movements fluid but deliberate, as if relearning her body. "The autopilot is locked on the colony's coordinates. Thirty years out." She glanced at him, a faint smirk tugging at her lips. "I'm guessing that's not where you want to go."

Yudai's expression hardened. "I definitely don't have thirty spare years. Can you override it?"

Amber moved through the cryo bay to the bridge. The bewildered looks of the surviving cowboys followed her. Reaching the main console, her fingers danced across the plastic keys on the navigation deck with ease. "While I was in the station's mainframe, I absorbed a lot - navigation protocols included. Give me a minute."

Yudai watched her work, the surreal nature of the moment slowly settling into something tangible. She was alive, in a way he hadn't dared to hope for. Yet as she tapped at the controls, he couldn't help but notice the subtle shifts in her expression - flashes of vulnerability amidst her focus.

Amber flexed her new fingers, the movements fluid but unnervingly precise. She stared at her reflection in a nearby console screen - a face both hers and not hers. Smooth, flawless skin. Eyes that gleamed faintly in the sterile light. She traced a hand along her cheek, the sensation muted yet vivid, as if her new body filtered the experience through an unseen veil.

Yudai stood behind her, his gaze heavy. "How does it feel?" he asked softly.

"This is my third body, I was also floating in the mainframe of that station" Amber replied, her voice tinged with bitterness. She turned to face him. "My idea of existence has changed. Am I Amber? I will never have her later memories, locked away in that QBS brain of hers. Am I just a facsimile of the original Amber?"

Yudai stepped closer, his brow furrowed. "You're alive, Amber. That's what matters." Her decanted chest rose and fell with a practiced breath, her programming mimicking a human habit she no longer needed. "Maybe that's enough for now."

The console's green light flashed, and the ship's hum shifted, signaling a course change.

"Done," she said, her tone lifting. Her confidence returned. "We're heading back to Earth."

Yudai felt the heaviness of the day's exertion. He sank onto the bench to the side of the console facing Amber, the hum of the pod's engines the only sound between them. He stared at his hands, still stained with the pink fluids of fallen synths, and let out a heavy sigh.

"We lost a lot of people, Amber. Almost lost you too. Was this all worth it?"

Amber's expression softened, her cool eyes narrowing slightly as if she were processing the weight of his words. She stepped closer, her movements unnaturally graceful yet somehow tentative. "It has to be," she said quietly. "If it wasn't, then what was the point of any of it?"

Yudai looked up at her, his face lined with exhaustion and something deeper – a grief he hadn't yet let himself feel. "You said your idea of existence has changed. Does that mean you believe this is enough?" His voice was low, but the question carried the weight of all his doubts.

Amber hesitated, her gaze flickering to the console as if searching for an answer in its blinking lights. "I don't know," she admitted, her voice barely above a whisper. "But I'm starting to think... maybe existence isn't about where we begin or how many versions of ourselves we leave behind. Maybe it's about what we fight for. Who we fight for."

Yudai leaned forward, his elbows on his knees, and ran a hand through his sweat-matted hair. "You're different now, Amber. Not just the body – everything. And I don't mean worse, or better. Just... different."

Amber tilted her head, considering his words. "So are you," she replied softly. Amber studied him, her crisp features softening. "When we met, you would've sacrificed anything - anyone - for the mission. Now... you're not so quick to make that call."

Yudai's jaw tightened, his eyes flicking to the floor. "You think I've gone soft?"

"No," Amber replied, her tone steady. "I think you've realized that people matter as much as the cause."

He was silent for a moment, the hum of the ship filling the space between them. Then he let out a dry, humorless chuckle. "People are what complicate the cause."

"And they're also what make it worth fighting for," Amber countered, her voice sharper now. "You didn't pull me off that station because it was tactical. You did it because you've finally stopped pretending that this fight is just strategy to you. You could have just left the bomb and gone."

Yudai looked at her then, his gaze heavy with the weight of years spent making impossible choices.

"Maybe. Or maybe I'm just tired of burying people."

Amber's lips quirked - not quite a smile, but something close. "Either way, it's a step forward."

He let her words sink in, the weight of them settling in his chest. "What's next?" he echoed, his tone caught between scepticism and hope.

"That's the question, isn't it?" Amber smiled faintly, her pale lips curving in a way that still felt entirely her. "We don't have all the answers yet. But we have a direction. And that's a start."

The silence between them wasn't uncomfortable. It carried the weight of their shared pain and the tentative threads of

237

hope, a shared comradery that connected them. The hum of the engines seemed to echo their thoughts, a steady rhythm in the vast unknown.

Amber sat beside him, her movements careful, as if she were still learning the nuances of her new body. She placed a hand on his, her touch cool but steady. "We survived, Yudai. Now we make new memories. That's enough for now."

He met her gaze, his shoulders relaxing slightly. "For now," he agreed, the corners of his mouth lifting into the faintest smile.

The vast void of space stretched out before them, an open expanse of uncertainty and possibility. Whatever lay ahead, they would face as a team – united by shared loss, unyielding resolve, and an unspoken bond that even death couldn't sever.

And as they settled in for the journey, a little blip on the flight deck pulsed – another Pod signal. They weren't the only ones to escape the station.